FANNY BLAKE, *woman&home*'s books editor, worked in publishing for many years before becoming a freelance journalist and author. She has written three novels including *Women of a Dangerous Age*. Her latest, *The Secrets Women Keep*, is out now.

FERN BRITTON is a TV presenter, novelist and, most recently, a star of *Strictly Come Dancing*. She is married to chef Phil Vickery and has four children. She has written three novels including *Hidden Treasures*. Her latest, *The Holiday Home*, is out now.

ELIZABETH BUCHAN is author of several novels including the prizewinning *Consider the Lily*, *Revenge of the Middle-Aged Woman* and *Daughters*. Her latest one, *A Thousand Little Lies*, which is set during the Second World War, will be published in 2014.

TRACY CHEVALIER moved to the UK from the US more than twenty years ago. She has since written seven novels, the most successful being *Girl With a Pearl Earring*, which was adapted into an Oscar-nominated film. Her latest book, *The Last Runaway* (HarperCollins), is out now.

JENNY COLGAN has written thirteen novels selling more than two and a half million copies, and recently won the Melissa Nathan Award for Comedy Romance for *Meet Me at the Cupcake Café*. The sequel, *Christmas at the Cupcake Café*, was published in 2012. Jenny lives in France with her husband and three children.

R. J. ELLORY is the author of the bestselling *A Quiet Belief in Angels*, which was a Richard and Judy Book Club selection in 2008. His work has been translated into twenty-three languages, and he was awarded the Theakston's Crime Novel of the Year for *A Simple Act of Violence*. R. J. Ellory is married with one son and lives in the UK. His most recent novel, *The Devil and the River*, is out now.

JULIA GREGSON is the prize-winning author of three novels, one book of non-fiction and several short stories. Her novel *East of the Sun* was chosen for the Richard and Judy Book Club and became a *Sunday Times* bestseller. Her most recent novel, *Jasmine Nights*, also a Richard and Judy Book Club selection, is a Second World War love story and is out now. Julia is married and lives in Wales.

TESSA HADLEY grew up in Bristol and trained as a teacher before taking a course in creative writing and publishing her first novel, *Accidents in the Home*, in 2002, which was longlisted for the *Guardian* First Book Award. She has since written four novels including *The London Train*, which was longlisted for the Orange Prize in 2011, and two collections of short stories. She lives in London with her husband Eric. Tessa teaches literature and creative writing at Bath Spa University. Her latest novel, *Clever Girl*, is out now.

MAEVE HARAN's debut novel, *Having it All*, became an international bestseller after it was published in 1991. She has written a further ten novels, one work of non-fiction, and two historical novels, including *The Painted Lady*, out now. Her latest book *The Time of Their Lives*, about the baby boomer generation refusing to grow old, will be out in 2014.

VERONICA HENRY began her career as a production secretary on *The Archers*, before becoming a screenwriter and working for many broadcasting legends including *Heartbeat* and *Holby City*. She lives with her husband and three sons on the North Devon coast, where she rents a beach hut every summer. She also loves riding on Exmoor. She is the author of numerous novels including the bestselling *The Long Weekend*. Her most recent book, *A Night on the Orient Express*, is out now.

VICTORIA HISLOP lives in Kent with her husband, journalist Ian Hislop, and their two children. Her first novel, *The Island*, became a bestseller after its publication in 2006, and she was awarded Newcomer of the Year at the Galaxy British Book Awards in 2007. Her latest novel, *The Thread*, is out now.

EOWYN IVEY grew up in Alaska, where she lives with her husband and two daughters. She works as a bookseller in a shop where she found her inspiration for her debut novel *The Snow Child*, which reached number five on the *Sunday Times* bestseller list.

CATHY KELLY is the author of many international number one bestsellers. Her novels are published all around the world. Cathy also has a passionate interest in children's rights and is an ambassador for UNICEF Ireland. Her role as a Global Parent sees her raising funds and awareness for children orphaned by or living with HIV/AIDS. She lives with her husband, their twin sons and their three dogs in Wicklow, Ireland.

ERIN KELLY was born in 1976. She grew up in Essex and read English at Warwick University. She has worked as a journalist since 1998, writing for newspapers and magazines including the *Telegraph*, the *Daily Mail*, *Red*, *Good Housekeeping*, *Marie Claire* and *woman&home*. Her short stories have been published in the *Sunday Times* and the *Sunday Express*. Her three novels, *The Poison Tree*, *The Sick Rose* and *The Burning Air* have been translated into eleven languages, and a fourth book is due for publication in 2014. Erin is married with two daughters and lives in north London, but yearns for the Suffolk coast where she spends most of her summers.

DEBORAH LAWRENSON spent her childhood moving around the world with Diplomatic Service parents, from Kuwait to China, Belgium, Luxembourg and Singapore. She graduated from Cambridge University and worked as a journalist in London. She is the author of five previous novels. Deborah is married with a daughter and lives in Kent. The family spends as much time as possible at a crumbling hamlet in Provence, France, the atmospheric setting for *The Lantern*, which was selected for the TV Book Club in 2011.

KATHY LETTE grew up in Sydney and wrote her first novel, *Puberty Blues*, when she was eighteen. Two years later it was made into a film, and Kathy has gone on to write a further twelve novels including the international bestsellers *Girls' Night Out* and *Mad Cows*. Kathy is married with two children and lives in London. Her latest novel, *The Boy Who Fell to Earth*, was inspired by Kathy's own personal experience of raising a son with autism.

LESLEY LOKKO had various careers, from cocktail waitress to kibbutz worker, before she trained as an architect. Several novels later, and as a full-time writer, Lesley splits her time between London, Johannesburg and Hastings. Her new novel, *Little White Lies*, is out now.

JILL MANSELL published her first novel, *Fast Friends*, in 1991. Since then she has published a further twenty-three books selling more than five million copies. She lives in Bristol with her partner and two children. Her latest novel is *Don't Want to Miss a Thing*.

VAL MCDERMID grew up in Kirkcaldy, Scotland. Her first novel, *Report for Murder*, was published in 1987, and her books have since become top-ten bestsellers. The ITV series *Wire in the Blood* was based on her character Dr Tony Hill. Her twenty-six books have sold more than ten million copies worldwide, and she has won numerous awards. Her latest novel, *The Vanishing Point*, is out now.

KATE MOSSE is the author of three works of non-fiction, three plays and six novels, including the number one multi-million international bestselling Languedoc Trilogy – *Labyrinth*,

Sepulchre and *Citadel* – published to outstanding reviews and sold in more than 40 countries throughout the world in 38 languages. Her standalone novel, *The Winter Ghosts*, was also a number one bestseller, confirming her position as one of our most captivating storytellers. Her collection of short stories, *The Mistletoe Bride & Other Ghostly Tales*, will be published in autumn 2013. In recognition of her services to literature, Kate was awarded an OBE in the Queen's Birthday Honours List in June 2013.

JOJO MOYES was born to artist parents who named her after a Beatles song. She was a journalist for ten years until she became a full-time novelist. The first of her nine novels was *Sheltering Rain*, published in 2002, and she has won the Romantic Novelists' Association Romantic Novel of the Year Award twice – in 2004 for *Foreign Fruit*, and in 2011 for *The Last Letter from Your Lover*. She lives on a farm in Essex with her journalist husband Charles Arthur and their three children. Her latest novel *The Girl You Left Behind* is out now.

ADELE PARKS grew up in the north of England and studied English at Leicester University. After graduating, she worked in advertising and management consultancy before publishing her first novel, *Playing Away*, in 2000. Since then she has written thirteen books, which have sold over two million copies in the UK alone, and she is translated into twenty-five languages. All her novels are *Sunday Times* top-ten bestsellers. She's spent much of her adult life in Italy, Botswana and London, but now lives in Guildford with her husband and son. *The State We're In* is out now.

NICKY PELLEGRINO's Italian father came to England and fell in love with a Liverpool girl. His mantra that you live to eat, not eat to live is one of the inspirations behind Nicky's delicious novels. Now living in New Zealand, where she works as a journalist, Nicky and her husband visit Italy to see family and eat the best mozzarella. Her latest novel, *The Food of Love Cookery School*, is out now.

IAN RANKIN is the bestselling author of the Inspector Rebus and Detective Malcolm Fox novels, as well as several stand-alone thrillers. He lives in Edinburgh, where his books are set, with his partner and two sons. His novel *Doors Open* was made into a major television drama and *Standing in Another Man's Grave* saw the much-anticipated return of Rebus. His latest novel, *Saints of the Shadow Bible*, is out in 2013.

CARA ROSS divides her time between a career in charity communications, her home on the beautiful Northumbrian coast and a writing shed in the garden funded by 'Fruitbat', her first attempt at writing fiction for publication, which won the Costa/*woman&home* short story prize in 2011. Cara is currently hard at work in the shed completing her first novel, *The Lavender House*, set in the Pelion region of Greece.

PENNY VINCENZI was a journalist before turning her hand to writing fiction full-time. Since her first novel, *Old Sins*, was published in 1989, she has written fourteen bestsellers and sold over eight million copies of her books worldwide. Penny divides her time between London and Gower, South Wales. Her latest novel, *The Decision*, is out now.

KATHERINE WEBB was born in 1977 and grew up in rural Hampshire before reading History at Durham University. Since then she has spent time in London and Venice, and now lives near Bath. Having worked as a waitress, au pair, personal assistant, bookbinder, library assistant, seller of fairy costumes and housekeeper, she now writes full-time. Her debut novel, *The Legacy*, was a Channel 4 Book Club pick for 2010 and won the overall popular vote. Her most recent novel, *The Misbegotten*, is out now.

Foreword

BY CATHERINE TATE

*I*t is my pleasure to introduce this year's collection of short stories by such a great range of writers who, like you, are supporting the work of Breast Cancer Care by the sale of this book. So first and foremost, thank you!

Hearing the devastating news that a loved one has breast cancer can make casualties of us all; it is a frightening and overwhelming time leaving many of us feeling vulnerable and at a loss as to what to do. Breast Cancer Care is there for us all. It is the only UK-wide charity dedicated to offering emotional and practical help to everyone affected by this life threatening illness not just the person diagnosed. Their helpline, website and online forums offer a friendly ear and support which can make a world of difference on a bad day.

For every book sold, Breast Cancer Care receives £1 towards these vital services which are all provided for free. A big thank you also goes to *woman&home* and its readers for supporting us for the past nine years and helping raise over £7,000,000.

Every day more people hear the news that they have breast cancer and you are helping to support them by buying this book. I hope you enjoy reading it. Maybe see you at the next Pink Ribbonwalk*? Come on, we're all in it together.

Anyone worried about breast cancer can visit Breast Cancer Care's helpful website www.breastcancercare.org.uk or call their free confidential helpline on 0808 800 6000

*Breast Cancer Care's Pink Ribbonwalks in association with *woman&home* are held every year during May and June. For details of these and other fundraising events visit www.breastcancer care.org/fundraising-events

the COFFEE SHOP Book Club

Stories by
KATE MOSSE, JOJO MOYES, IAN RANKIN,
PENNY VINCENZI, KATHERINE WEBB
and many more . . .

EDITED BY FANNY BLAKE FOR
woman&home

An Orion Paperback
First published in Great Britain in 2013
by Orion Books
an imprint of the Orion Publishing Group Ltd
Orion House, 5 Upper St Martin's Lane,
London, WC2H 9EA

An Hachette UK company

3 5 7 9 10 8 6 4 2

A CIP catalogue record for this book
is available from the British Library.

ISBN 978 1 4091 2974 5

Typeset at The Spartan Press Ltd,
Lymington, Hants

Printed in Great Britain by Clays Ltd, St Ives plc

The Orion Publishing Group's policy is to use papers
that are natural, renewable and recyclable products and
made from wood grown in sustainable forests. The logging
and manufacturing processes are expected to conform to
the environmental regulations of the country of origin.

www.orionbooks.co.uk

Contents

Letting Go

BY FANNY BLAKE

*T*wenty-five years of marriage. Not bad. No, better than that. A wonderful, happy achievement. Or would have been, if Tom had only lived to see it.

The joke (a bad one) was that he had been at the leisure centre when he died, eight long years ago. Clare had always viewed the place with suspicion. Rightly, as it turned out. He had been on the running machine when he keeled over. Dead by the time the ambulance arrived. That had been some time before she had been tracked down to the farm where she was cajoling a cow through a difficult labour. Professional to the ends of her rubber-gloved fingers, she had to wait for the birth before she made her terrible journey to the hospital.

Tom would have laughed if he'd known. Instead, he was lying in the mortuary, pale and cold as marble, waiting for her. Her determination not to let him down was what had got her through those initial pain-fuelled months. That and Mel, who was only nine when it happened. Clare still felt the agony of seeing their daughter's small face tilted towards her as she asked when Dad was coming home, and of her own inability to answer.

Tom always had such a robust attitude towards life and death. One of the things she loved about him. 'We're born, we die. It happens.'

But not yet, a voice inside her had screamed, and continued to scream, for a long time. Somehow she had found the inner strength she needed to cope and, over the following years, the character of her grief changed until it became a reluctant acceptance. She had thrown herself into her work at the veterinary practice, and into the business of bringing up an increasingly bolshy young teenager.

This anniversary could be both celebration and opportunity for some much-needed family bonding. She would inveigle their prickly seventeen-year-old daughter into coming away with her for a long weekend, during which they would remember Tom together. They rarely spoke of him now. In fact, they rarely spoke to one another at all.

After spending weeks delving into the attractions of different city breaks, Clare settled on Granada in southern Spain. After their never-to-be-forgotten honeymoon, she and Tom had often talked about returning there, but they never had. What better time than this?

When invited to come, Mel's reaction had been predictable. 'How am I supposed to know what I'm doing in May?'

'But I'd like you to come.'

Clare could see from the pout – a frequent weapon of choice – how much the idea appealed. 'Mum, I'll try, but I've got exams in June, and it's Emma's birthday on the second . . .'

'I'm only talking about four days. That's all.'

'Maybe. I'll have to check with Matt. I'll let you know.'

Clare sighed. Matt had been Mel's on-off boyfriend for a year now. Their relationship, which veered between the dizzy heights of romantic love and despair with what was becoming monotonous regularity, was a mystery to her. In fact, so was her daughter. Theirs had become a relationship of delicate negotiation, one in which eggshells were frequently trodden on.

She glanced at her laptop, at the pictures of Granada left open in the hope of seducing Mel. On that honeymoon, Tom had bought her Washington Irving's *Tales of the Alhambra*. Where was the book now? Had she lost it deliberately because of the memories it evoked? The photo of the fortress at sunset whispered to her of ghosts and legends, including her favourite, the Rose of Alhambra, who wept for the faithlessness of man.

Ghosts.

Her daydream fractured as Blue, their leggy young lurcher, skedaddled towards a knock at the back door, barking. On the doorstep, she found her friend Jenny struggling to get off her wellies. Having freed her second foot, she followed Clare into the kitchen. Soon, they were sitting at the long pine table, mugs of tea and a tartan tin of biscuits between them, the day's post and newspaper pushed to one side.

'What's this?' Jenny pulled the laptop towards her. 'Looks amazing. What are you planning? Not you and Nick? Already?'

After a drink and a couple of meals out together, Nick, a recently divorced local farmer, was obviously hoping their relationship would develop. Clare recollected their kisses. Perhaps it would.

'Bit soon for that,' she said hastily, thinking of the speed of small-town gossip. 'I do like him, but he's a bit insistent. No, I thought I'd celebrate Tom's and my anniversary with Mel. A family thing.'

Jen reached across the table to put her hand over Clare's. 'Oh, Clare. I thought you'd moved on.'

Clare withdrew her hand sharply. 'I have, but whatever happens, I won't forget Tom. I don't want to. He's Mel's dad. The idea was to make a girls' weekend out of it and remember him together.'

'And she's said no.' Jenny knew them too well.

'Mel's got her own life now. I shouldn't have expected otherwise.' Clare often found herself making excuses for her daughter. She picked out a Jammie Dodger, hesitated, then put it back.

'I'd come with you, but I couldn't, not without Brian. He'd go mad.' Jenny's husband kept her on an unenviably short leash. 'Why don't you go on your own?'

'No way. I wouldn't know what to do with myself.'

Later that night, Clare lay awake, mulling over their

4

conversation. She had *come to terms* (how she hated that phrase) with Tom's death. She hadn't locked herself inside her grief, but had involved herself in the community, as much as doubling up as a vet and a mother would allow.

Eventually despairing of ever finding an available single man, she had trawled various online dating sites. Some of the men had been sad and lonely, and dragged her down to their level of disappointment. Others, such as Roger, a dentist from Swindon and Jack, a haulage company owner, had been great. She had danced, drunk and had fun with them. She'd made noisy love in hotel rooms and shared secretive moments of passion at home, anxious about waking Mel. And now there was Nick. But none of them had replaced Tom. Not yet. Mel had vetted each and every one, raising an eyebrow or screwing up her nose, making her distaste obvious.

Of course her daughter didn't want to travel with her. Would she have wanted to accompany her own mother on holiday? Perhaps Jen had a point, and she should break with habit and go alone.

The following evening, after a draining morning of consultations and an afternoon of minor ops and a visit to a mare in foal, Clare sat down in the kitchen with her laptop.

'What are you doing?' Mel leaned over her shoulder and peered at the screen.

Clare bit back her reproof about the acrid tang of cigarette smoke in Mel's hair. How many times had they had the smoking conversation? She was too exhausted to have it again.

'Looks wicked.' A deep-green-varnished fingernail pointed at a narrow, white-walled street in Granada's old town. 'But where's the sea, the sangria? Isn't that why people go to Spain?'

'Not me,' Clare returned firmly. Bikini-clad beach days had lost their appeal the moment she'd lost her waist. 'No. I want to go back and show you where we started out together. Dad would have liked that.'

'Pity he didn't stick around then.' Mel's interest had wandered on to a celebrity magazine.

'*Mel!* That's an awful thing to say.' But Clare had heard the anger in her daughter's voice. Anger she hadn't realised Mel still felt. 'What do you mean?'

Mel turned a page and her voice wobbled. 'He should have looked after himself better, shouldn't he? He had us to think about.'

Clare looked at her daughter. 'I can't believe you just said that.'

'Well, I did.' Mel spoke slowly. 'And I'll decide about the holiday later.'

Clare fought to be reasonable. Normal. 'The prices will go up if we leave it. Do come. I don't want you remembering Dad like that.'

But the only response was the sound of Mel's footsteps on the stairs.

Clare scrolled down to stare at the Court of the Lions, remembering wandering through the arched gallery with Tom, holding hands. She looked down at her wedding ring. Suddenly her mind was made up. She would go on her own.

As the day of departure drew nearer, so Clare's reluctance about travelling alone deepened. She had asked Mel to join her again, casually, but hoping for the right answer.

'Look, Mum, I can't. There's a gig that weekend that Matt says we mustn't miss. Take Nick.' But they both knew that wasn't going to happen. Not this time.

On the day itself, Mel wasn't even there to say goodbye. Something else had prior claim on her time. Pushing her disappointment in her daughter to one side, Clare caught the train to the airport.

On the plane, she had time to reflect. Mel wasn't a bad girl. Perhaps it was time they started to let each other go. This would be a rite of passage. If she didn't speak to anyone for four days, she'd survive. She'd explore, she'd read, she'd go to bed early. And when she came home, Mel would be pleased to see her and Nick would be waiting. She was surprised by a flutter of pleasure at the thought.

She wheeled her hand luggage towards Arrivals, the bright spring day a relief from the wind and rain she'd left behind. Suddenly she felt unaccountably nervous, and dug in her bag for the piece of paper with the name of the hotel.

In her room, she poured herself a gin and tonic from the minibar and lay on the bed. She jumped when the phone rang.

'Mrs Collins? I have a message for you.'

'A message?' Alarm bells sounded. Either something had happened to Mel, or there was an emergency at the practice.

'A taxi will be picking you up for dinner at eight thirty.'

She must have misheard. 'A taxi?' she repeated. Dinner?

'It's booked in the name of Nick Johnston.' The concierge hung up.

Nick! He couldn't have. Their relationship had moved on to another level, but he knew why she had come to Granada. It was completely inappropriate for him to turn up uninvited. She knocked back her drink. She couldn't cope if he was jealous of Tom. She wouldn't meet him. She poured another, smaller gin. Yes she would, and she wouldn't mince her words.

By eight thirty, she was ready. A pashmina over the shoulders of her smart blouse and jeans, she stepped into the waiting taxi. She watched the street life through the windows, every minute more excited to be there, anxious to get this over with.

Walking through the tapas bar, hectic with customers shouting their orders over the counter, she was shown into a restaurant. She looked around at the other diners before being shown to her table. He must be in the candlelit annexe.

The maître d' showed her through. Nick was obviously late. Another black mark.

At one table, a young woman sat alone. As Clare

approached she looked up, a smile spreading across her face.

Clare stared at her in disbelief. 'Mel! But the gig . . . Nick?'

'That fell through weeks ago, so I decided to surprise you. Nick helped. I borrowed his name for the taxi. Was that awful?'

Stunned, Clare took her seat.

'I couldn't let you celebrate the anniversary on your own.' Mel held out the tourist guide she'd been reading. 'And I've found an amazing spa quite near the hotel. Look.'

Wiping away a tear, Clare burst out laughing, then leaned over and kissed her daughter's cheek.

The Surprise Gift

BY FERN BRITTON

*J*enni took a final look around her daughter's bedroom and shut the door. For the past week she had been a slave to lists, laundry and vacuuming. And now Christmas was almost here.

Her husband, Roger, was out collecting her mum and dad from Plymouth, and the twins, Tom and Flick, were arriving by train the next day.

She walked down the worn wooden stairs of their Cornish home and admired her Christmas tree. It was missing the little fairy on top that Flick had made in Year Four. But family tradition said that only Flick could put her up there on Christmas Eve.

Jenni couldn't wait to have her family around her. Unable to resist fiddling with the fairy lights, she was reorganising them when the phone rang.

'Hi, Mum. It's me.' Flick. 'I'm phoning to say we're not getting the train.'

'What?' Jenni's heart plummeted.

'No. We're getting a lift. From a friend.'

'As long as you're still coming.'

'Yes, of course we are! The thing is . . .' She

hesitated. 'I've asked him if he'd like to spend Christmas with us. Can he?'

Jenni thought about the bed situation.

'I could make up a camp bed in Tom's room.'

Flick was silent, then, 'Yeah. That'll be cool. Thanks. We'll see you about four. Love you, Mum.'

Jenni spent the next hour hunting out the camp bed.

'Hellooo!' called Roger from downstairs. 'Your mum and dad are here, and it's snowing.'

Jenni smoothed the pillow on the makeshift bed and went to the top of the stairs. She saw with fondness the tops of her parents' greying heads. Her mother looked up.

'Roger drove very well, given the weather.'

Roger looked up at Jenni and gave her a knowing wink. Her parents always liked to comment on Roger's driving, and the road conditions. It was a conversation that would keep them going through most of Christmas.

Jenni walked downstairs and hugged them before getting them settled in front of the fire. Then she remembered Flick's phone call.

'No need to collect the kids from the station tomorrow. They're getting a lift down with one of Tom's mates.'

'Not in this weather?' said her mother.

'Yes, Mum. But they'll be here before it's dark.'

'Can I watch the news?' Her father reached for the remote control.

She passed it to him and let him enjoy his armchair view of the world.

The following morning, Christmas Eve, Jenni was awake early. She wanted to get into Padstow to pick up some last bits of shopping.

Roger put their tray of morning tea on the chest of drawers and stood next to her. In the harbour, the boats were drifted in snow. The seagulls skated crazily across the frozen water.

'Come back into bed for a bit, maid. My feet are freezing.'

Snuggled up together and drinking the steaming tea, the two of them discussed what last-minute things needed doing. Then Roger asked, 'Who's this bloke driving them down, then?'

'Someone from uni, I suppose.'

'Penniless student looking for cheap lodgings and food, probably.'

Jenni dug him in the ribs. 'He might take you out for a pint if you ask 'im.'

By three o'clock, flurries of snow were blowing in. 'You'll not be going to church tonight, will you, Jen?' asked her father. 'Not in this weather.'

'Dad, it's just a five-minute walk. We'll wrap up warm.'

'I don't want your mother to slip.'

'I won't slip. I'm perfectly fine on my legs.'

Jenni slid out of the room, leaving them to it.

By four o'clock the sun had set, and just as Jenni started to fret there was a knock and, outside, voices sang 'Once In Royal David's City'. She flung open the door, and there were Tom and Flick. She hugged them and got them inside before turning to their mystery friend. He was tall, very thin, with long, unbrushed hair, and looked seven or eight years older than Tom and Flick.

'Mum, this is Ax,' said Flick, holding on to his arm.

Jenni held out her hand.

'Hello. Nice to meet you.'

The tall stranger loomed into the hall without saying a word. He shrugged off his battered leather jacket to reveal several tattoos of hell-abiding demons.

Jenni and Roger glanced at each other.

'And this is Granny and Grandad.'

Flick was in the sitting room introducing everybody when Tom bounded into the room.

'Ax, Dad fancies a pint. D'you want to join us?'

Ax looked anxiously towards Jenni, who smiled.

'Yeah. Get on. As long as you're back for midnight mass.'

The three men left the house, letting in an icy swirl of air.

'Who is he?' asked Granny, leaning over towards Flick.

'He's a friend of ours.'

'Looks like a druggie to me,' said her grandmother suspiciously.

Flick hooted with laughter. 'Well, he's not!'

'Here you are, Mum.' Jenni gave her mother a small glass of sherry.

'Thank you, dear.' She sipped it. 'This'll give me an appetite for supper.'

Flick got up from her position on the floor by her grandmother. 'I'll help, Mum.' Jenni mouthed a silent thank you.

Jenni and Flick busied themselves getting all they needed on to the scrubbed wooden table.

'What do you think of Ax?' Flick asked, carefully cutting thin slices of bread.

Jenni recognised the need for diplomacy. 'He seems very nice. Quiet. How did Tom meet him?'

'Actually, he's my friend. We met when I was travelling in the summer.'

Jenni didn't think she was going to like what she heard next.

'He's my boyfriend.'

Jenni rested the knife she was using on the sprouts. 'Oh.'

'Is that a problem? Because of the way he looks? Or that he's a bit older than me?'

Jenni looked at her beautiful daughter and tried to smile. 'No, no. He's just . . . not your type, maybe.'

'You are so judgemental.' Flick's eyes blazed from under the lock of blonde hair that had fallen forward over her face.

'That's not what I meant.' Jenni started on the sprouts again. 'As long as he makes you happy.'

'He does.' Flick found two willow-pattern plates and arranged the sandwiches.

'I'll take these in to Gran and Grandad.'

Jenni was left to finish the Christmas lunch preparations. The turkey was good and fat and, as she was seasoning it, Flick returned with the empty plates. Sliding them into the sink, she said, 'By the way, Ax is vegetarian.'

Jenni stopped what she was doing.

'What?'

'Vegan, actually, but he'll love the veg. Just don't roast the spuds in dripping.'

Jenni took another deep breath. 'Right. I wish you'd told me earlier.'

'It's no big deal, is it? In fact, my New Year's resolution is to stop eating meat.'

Jenni took another deep breath. 'Good for you.'

On her way out of the room, Flick added, 'And Mum, no need for the camp bed. Ax will sleep in my room, with me.'

As soon as she'd gone, Jenni found a tumbler and poured herself a good slug of cream sherry. She opened the back door and stood on the snowy step, a small tear of hurt and frustration on her cheek.

When the boys got back from the pub, only Roger noticed her slight tipsiness.

He put his hands on her shoulders.

'Are you all right, love?'

'Absolutely fine. Ax doesn't eat meat, he's sleeping

with our daughter and I'm a judgemental fascist. Yep, I'm absolutely fine.'

He hugged her.

'We'll get through it. He's not so bad, just a bit shy. He's coming to church though, which must be a good sign.'

In the hall, Tom and Flick were helping their grandparents into their coats. Jenni saw that her father looked pale. 'You don't have to come if you're tired, Dad.'

He looked at her, annoyed.

'I've never missed church on Christmas Eve and I don't intend to now.'

He took hold of his wife's arm and together they ventured out into the wintry night. Jenni found that a path had been cleared through the snow.

'Tom and Ax did that when we came home from the pub,' murmured Roger.

The church was filling up, but they found a side pew with a good view of the altar. Jenni sat next to her father. They knelt together and she gave a short prayer.

'Please God, don't let Flick marry Ax. Thank you. Amen.'

When she looked up, her father was struggling to sit back on the bench, sounding breathless.

'Indigestion,' he wheezed. 'Must be that cheese and pickle sandwich.'

Jenni rummaged in her bag and found a mint. 'Here, Dad. This might help.'

He winked as he took it with his gnarled fingers and popped it in his mouth.

The organ struck up and the service began. The family sang with gusto, giving real welly to the much-loved carols.

Jenni looked towards the end of the pew and noticed Ax, sitting silent, looking with a keen eye at her father. She followed his gaze to see her father clutching his right arm, then slumping slowly on to the bench. His lips were turning blue.

'Dad,' she said quickly, sitting down beside him. 'Dad!'

A long arm in a battered leather jacket reached across to support her father as he threatened to slip to the floor.

'Flick! Call an ambulance. Roger, help me lie him in the aisle,' said Ax urgently.

Jenni watched with horrible fascination as Ax removed his jacket to place it under her father's head. The people in the pews around them had stopped singing to gawp. The organ fell silent. Ax was compressing the old man's chest, counting, then asking Tom to check for a pulse in his grandfather's neck.

Jenni's mother was kneeling on the tiled floor and stroking her father's hand, whispering his name.

Eventually, an ambulance crew arrived and took over. Ax was talking to them and they listened with respect. As they took her father out of the church, strapped to a small wheelchair, the rest of the family followed.

Outside, the twirling blue lights of the ambulance lit up the graveyard. Roger offered to get the car so that they could follow the ambulance to Truro.

Jenni watched as Ax helped her mother into the ambulance, then stepped in after her. The doors closed on them and the ambulance set off.

'Mum,' Flick's tear-stained face attempted a reassuring smile. 'Ax is brilliant at what he does. Grandad's in good hands.'

'I don't understand.' Jenni blinked. 'Why did he go with Dad?'

'He's a doctor. I met him in Jordan. He's been working with the Syrian refugees.'

The night was a long one. Jenni and her family waited in the relatives' room until the small hours. At last, Ax, dressed in borrowed scrubs, came to find them.

'They let me into theatre. I've been with him all the time. Everything's gone well. He's asleep now – something you all need. Go home. I'll stay here until you get back.'

They postponed Christmas until 4 January, when the patient was allowed home. Ax and Roger supported him as he walked up the path, past all the Welcome Home bunting and balloons put up by Jenni and Flick.

Once her father was settled in the sitting room, Jenni went to put the kettle on. Ax was already sitting at the kitchen table.

'Cup of tea?' she asked.

'Yes, please. No milk.'

She looked at this quiet, scruffy man.

'I want to thank you, Ax, for everything. And I owe you an apology for . . .'

He looked at her.

'For . . . Well, for . . . mistaking you for . . . someone you're not.'

He smiled. 'My mum hates the way I look, if that's what you mean.'

She went over to him and hugged his lanky frame. 'Thank you.'

They heard Flick calling from the other room.

'Mum. Ax. Come into the lounge.'

Roger was standing holding Flick's ancient home-made fairy. He helped Flick on to a small stool by the Christmas tree.

She turned to address the small gathering.

'Welcome home, Grandad. We've been waiting for this.'

She took the little fairy and, reaching up, placed her carefully on the tallest spike of the sparkling tree. She turned again.

'Happy Christmas, everybody!'

Extra Time

BY ELIZABETH BUCHAN

*M*imi's voice on the phone is muffled and desperate. 'Liddy, you've got to help me. Ten extras have flu, the agency can't supply any more and the director's going ape. Can you come? My job is on the line . . .'

'An extra in a film?'

Liddy is between cases and undergoing a professional wobble of confidence. This last one has been an exhausting battle to keep a Somalian refugee in the country, which she has lost, and she is licking her wounds at home. She is also mourning the departure of David. At the beginning of the case, he packed his bags and told her that they were not compatible, and anyway, even after ten years together, he wasn't sure that he'd ever got through to 'the real Liddy'.

Whatever that meant.

Life without David is duller and harder. Far more of a slog. Although it had been hard to handle at times, she misses the see-saw of emotions – elation, pain and, surprisingly often, robust contentment.

'Liddy? Come on. You can't be serious and human-rightsy all the time. I'm your best friend, and I'm in trouble.'

'OK,' she says.

Mimi snaps into professional assistant-director mode. 'Be here in an hour. Tell them you're from Haycraft's Extras if asked, and that you worked on my last film. If Wardrobe contacts you, say your hair isn't dyed. I will ignore you totally. No mobiles on set. Got it?'

Five minutes later, Mimi sends a text: *Director thinks he's Leonardo and Scorsese rolled into one. Happy days. Xxx*

Her hair piled up around a hairpiece, Liddy is dressed in a corset, a satin petticoat and a tight, sprigged muslin overdress with a plunging neckline. The ensemble is finished off by a pair of red shoes and a flamboyant hat adorned with plumes and revolutionary cockade in red, white and blue. She is waiting with a group of extras on the set, which is a remarkable facsimile of the Place de la Concorde in Paris in 1791.

'Last week I was a hobbit . . .'

A woman beside her is regaling some of the first-timers with her extra history.

The film is set during the French Revolution, and its story centres on a pair of minor royals who initially supported the Revolution only to become two of its most notorious victims.

Today, the extras are to be people at the bloody scene of their execution. Their instructions are to boo

as the unfortunate pair climb the steps to the guillotine, and to cheer when their heads thud into the
basket. Afterwards, buoyed up by the slaughter, the
extras are to dance in the streets.

If the unfamiliar corset leaves Liddy a little breathless, the sensation of skirts sweeping around her legs is,
paradoxically, rather exciting. Her body feels quite
different. Its points of reference – the plunging neckline, the tumbling hair, the hidden legs – shift her
centre of gravity. She points a foot and swishes the
material around her ankles, and discovers that she is
more than a little intrigued by this journey back into
the past.

Minutes pass, then an hour, while a camera track is
built around a business-like replica of a guillotine. The
film crew busy themselves and ignore the extras.

In the distance, she spots Mimi whisking about with
a clipboard. After an hour and a half, there is a ripple of
expectation as the woman-who-had-been-a-hobbit
announces that things are about to happen.

They don't.

Liddy sighs audibly.

'Nothing like a good piece of butchery to set you up
for the day.'

The man who has come to stand beside Liddy has
longish hair tied back with a black ribbon, a floppy
shirt, cravat, waistcoat and breeches. Mid-fortyish,
perhaps, not particularly handsome, the costume
doesn't sit well on him. He extends a hand. 'Can I
introduce myself? Currently, I am the non-speaking

Comte de Sevigny but I allow my friends to call me Will. I am shortly to be beheaded.' He takes in the hat, the skirts, the hair . . . the artful construct that is Liddy for the day. Clearly, he likes what he sees and sketches a mock bow. 'Actually, I would like you to be my countess.'

Hot colour dyes her cheeks. 'Thank you. My name is Liddy.'

'Liddy.' He rolls the name around his tongue. 'Doesn't go with the outfit. You look more like a . . . a Marie-Hélène.'

Liddy is beginning to feel that the present and the past are in danger of becoming muddled – but very enjoyably. 'Marie-Hélène? I like it.'

'Marie-Hélène, then.'

'Do you do this often?'

He shrugs. 'In my youth, I wanted to be an actor. It didn't work. But from time to time, I take a day off and allow myself a little make-believe. *Nostalgie* . . . as the Comte de Sevigny might say.' Again the smile hits his eyes. 'But I had no idea that my life would be at stake.'

Liddy gestures to the guillotine. This is being given its final touches by the baseball-capped crew, who are splashing fake blood over the straw and piling heads into the basket. Looming above them with aggressive intent, it is very convincing.

She takes a gulp of fresh air and the corset squeezes her waist. 'I'm a lawyer,' she informs Will. 'Human rights. I've spent my working life fighting repression. I never imagined I'd spend a fun afternoon profiting from it.'

'But don't you anyway? Profit from oppression?'

One eyebrow raised, he is looking directly at Liddy – with the result that she has the oddest feeling that he can read her hidden sorrows.

'You're right.'

'I should know,' he confesses. 'I work for an African charity.'

Now she looks at him. What does she see? Someone who has made the best of early setbacks?

'So . . .' He falls back into character and adjusts the lace on his cuffs. 'You wouldn't defend me, wicked aristo that I am? You will watch me die with a song on your lips?'

Stung, she is about to give a detailed reply as to why human-rights lawyers are vital. She ducks her head and the plumes in her extravagant hat tickle her cheek. This makes Liddy laugh, and she jettisons the serious argument.

'Even aristos have rights.'

He nods. 'Good to know as I die. Well, goodbye, Marie-Hélène. I have to go and take up my position. I'm afraid you won't see me again in this world.'

'It's a far, far better thing that you do.'

'Harsh. This . . .' he indicates the pair of them, '. . . is a far, far better thing, I think. But if I have to lose my head during an afternoon's work, so be it.'

He raises a hand and moves off towards the others waiting at the entrance to the set.

Liddy does something very peculiar. Why, she will never know but she lifts her skirts and sketches a curtsey.

Professionally mud-stained and dishevelled, the minor French royals emerge from their green rooms and are helped up into the tumbril. Will and a couple of others climb in behind them and their hands are tied behind their backs.

The tumbril creaks over the fake cobbles into the Place de la Concorde and stops. Off the set, one of the crew holds up a placard with the word NOISE written on it.

The extras let rip.

'Cut.'

All action slithers to a halt. The tumbril is in the wrong place.

Half an hour drags by. They begin again.

'Cut.'

The doomed female royal has wept too hard and her mascara has run.

'For God's sake,' comes over the megaphone. 'Someone tell her what to do.'

Liddy feels the creep of hunger and exhaustion steal over her, the debilitation of anxiety and, almost, of fear.

Again.

'Cut.'

This time . . . ?

This time, Will mounts the wooden steps to the

platform. The soldiers of the Republic seize him and appear to handle him so roughly her stomach lurches.

Don't hurt him. The crowd surges forward. The executioner steps up and unbuttons Will's shirt. The hairs on the back of Liddy's neck stand up.

This is a film set, for God's sake. Artificial. Creaking. Nonsensical, even. Yet there is something terrifying and horrible about the alive and vital Will poised above the baying crowd. Constricted under her costume, her heart shudders with empathy for the grief and shock that must have been endured by those who had lived through these events.

'No,' she hears herself crying out. 'No!'

Does he hear her? He glances in her direction. Liddy's hands fly to her cheeks. Then he is thrown on to the plank and the blade comes whooshing down. The executioner steps forward and pulls a head out of the basket.

But Liddy won't look. It's as if all the years of serious application and striving, of loss and mistakes, of struggling to save her clients from injustice, are surging to the surface. Hobbled by her skirts, she stands still among the crowing crowd of extras while tears pour down her cheeks.

The woman-who-was-a-hobbit nudges her – and it isn't a friendly gesture. 'What on earth do you think you're doing? Don't let His Lordship see you. We'll have to do it again.'

Later, the extras are tutored in the steps for the ten-second, triumphant street dance after the hero and heroine have met their end.

Two fiddlers take up a stance by the guillotine and the men line up opposite the women. Liddy is being partnered by a ruffian in striped culottes and red Phrygian cap, and has abandoned her own hat. The fiddlers play a wild and lively jig. Liddy's spirits rise and her feet begin to tap on the fake cobbles.

The men advance towards the women and turn them around. Feet fly through the bloodied straw and over the pools of gore. The music grows wilder and faster. The women join hands and gallop around the men bunched in the centre of the circle . . .

'Cut.'

The dance makes Liddy – already light-headed from emotion – doubly so.

'CUT.'

Round they go again.

Who cares? The music flows through her from the top of her coiffured head to her revolutionary shod feet.

'IT'S A WRAP, PEOPLE.'

Liddy comes to a standstill. She is panting and exhausted, and wants to laugh and cry all at the same time.

The director is satisfied and the extras are dismissed. Back in the trailer, Liddy sheds her skirts with regret. Her hair is unpinned and her corset unlaced. The image reflected back from the mirror is of the familiar

Liddy . . . she leans forwards to study it. *Marie-Hélène?*

Who is the real Liddy? The one who said to David, 'Do what you want' and had never spoken to him again? Or the one who waited until he had left before weeping until she was stupefied?

In her black skirt and white T-shirt, bag over her arm, Liddy emerges. A crowd of crew and extras are milling about. Holding her bag tight, Liddy makes for the exit.

'There you are,' says a voice.

She swings round. 'But your hair is short.'

Indeed, the long hair caught back in a ribbon has vanished. In its place is brown hair of nondescript cut. It suits him better. So do the jeans and leather jacket. 'The art of wiggery,' he says. 'It does wonders.'

At that moment, the guillotine is dragged back off the set and there is a cry of 'Watch it!' The woman-who-was-a-hobbit is not fast enough moving out of the way and she stumbles into Liddy. Instantly, Will catches her. For a moment, his hand rests on her waist and, as if she is still encased in the corset, Liddy gasps for breath.

Will removes his hand and she is acutely conscious of its absence.

'We didn't make it in the other life,' he says. 'But there is this one.'

From the roots of her freshly combed hair to the soles of her plimsolled feet, a wild, sweet elation drowns Liddy.

Grandmother's Garden

BY TRACY CHEVALIER

*R*uth could not understand why, at the end of her life, her mother chose to be covered by such an ugly quilt. Mildred had made it sixteen years before, when Ruth was pregnant with her daughter Stella. The patchwork pattern was called 'Grandmother's Garden', which Ruth had learned to make when she was a girl. Her mother had taught her to cut out hexagonal paper templates, baste fabric around them, then sew rosettes formed by six hexagons ringing a seventh. For this quilt, Mildred had used browns, greens, oranges and yellows, a straightforward homage rather than an ironic nod to the 1970s.

The quilt was one of a handful of things Mildred had requested for her room in the nursing home, back when she could still speak: a photograph of the family taken when Ruth was young, a pair of plaid slippers, an old bottle of lily-of-the-valley eau de cologne.

It was hard these days to look at her mother. Mildred's face was so thin, her skin so translucent that it was like watching a living skull. Her eyes were mostly vacant, though swimming to their pale blue surface now and then was a primitive urge dispatched from some far corner of her mind, to flail briefly before sinking down again. Her mouth was the only part of her face that moved much now; it alternately grimaced and pouted like a yogic exercise gone awry. It was this, and those helpless flashes in her placid eyes, that drove Ruth to study the quilt instead, despite its drab colours and insistent, uninspired pattern.

Her mother had made quilts years before when Ruth was young, and took up the pastime again when she discovered she was going to have a grandchild. After making a small cot quilt for Stella, also a 'Grandmother's Garden', she kept on making rosettes, and eventually had enough to sew a cover for the single bed in the spare room. As far as Ruth knew, Mildred had never used the quilt herself, so it was odd that she should ask for it to be part of the bare-bones end of her life.

Today her daughter had accompanied Ruth to the nursing home. Stella was slumped in a chair in the corner, ears plugged into headphones, tapping away at her phone faster than Ruth had ever imagined thumbs could move. She had heard that teenagers' thumb muscles were growing abnormally large. Stella never looked up from her hand-sized entertainment centre, blocking out the room so effectively that Ruth wondered why she had agreed to visit her grandmother at all. Well, not exactly *agreed*: she had simply not said no when Ruth suggested it. Ruth had learned that the lack of an argument was the best she could expect from a fifteen-year-old.

Grandmother and granddaughter couldn't be more different. Mildred was of a generation who took great care with appearance and behaviour. Until her mind began to go, she had her hair washed and set every week, though it had become hard to find hairdressers who could do it. She wore blusher and the same coral shade of lipstick all her life. Her jewellery was also spare – clip-on pearl earrings and a flat gold chain. Her hemlines were modest, her heels the sensible height favoured by the Queen. Mildred's house had been full of things such as lint rollers, lavender water for ironing, silver polish and several different bottles of stain remover. Unlike many households – unlike Ruth's – she had used all of these things.

She was very particular about looking after her shoes, regularly re-heeling them and using shoe trees to keep their shape. When Stella was little, Mildred had taught her how to use shoe polish, and Stella had gone through a brief phase of wearing the cleanest, shiniest shoes to school. Now when Ruth timidly pointed to the scuffs and mud on Stella's boots, her daughter smirked.

Stella's ripped jeans rode low to reveal the muffin-top bulge so common in teenage girls – if they weren't starving themselves. Her bra straps showed through her shirts. Her long hair was straggly with split ends, and she never had it cut except when she took scissors to it herself to produce a fringe that was too short. She wore bright eye shadow and an abundance of jewellery – necklaces tangled together, bangles up her arms, the obligatory multiple piercings in her ears. More was more, as far as Stella was concerned.

Mildred was forthright in her criticism of Stella, and unlike Ruth she was not afraid to tell her granddaughter directly.

'That fringe is dreadful. At least you know now you'll never be a hairdresser.'

'Take those headphones off when I'm speaking to you, dear. It's unbearably rude.'

'That blouse makes you look like a barmaid. Is that all you're planning to do with your life?'

'Enunciate, dear. Then you might sound a little cleverer than you are.'

To Ruth's surprise, Stella absorbed these zingers without a fight, and seemed to like her grandmother the more for it. Not that you'd know it now, with Stella doing everything she could to absent herself from the room. Ruth studied her daughter. Among the cheap tat from the high street looped around Stella's neck, she spotted a strand of seed pearls Mildred had given her granddaughter one Christmas. There were other gifts – a cloth for polishing silver jewellery, padded hangers for dresses, a beaded black clutch – that sat at the back of a cupboard but which Ruth suspected Stella would use some day. Give her a few years.

Her daughter looked up, caught her mother's eye and made a face. Maybe ten years.

Ruth turned back to her mother. Mildred bared her teeth and scrabbled her birdlike fingers among the orange and green rosettes.

'Maw,' she groaned. She had lived an orderly life, and would be mortified to see the personal chaos she had descended to that no teeth-whitening sticks or stain removers or Mason Pearson hairbrushes could keep under control.

No one had warned Ruth about the exhaustion of witnessing approaching death, about the anger and boredom and anxiety mixed together, and how none of these feelings made any difference. Your mother died in a timeline established by her body, and there was nothing you could do about it.

It was all so tiring. Ruth closed her eyes. She just wanted to lie down.

Her daughter's music changed from tinny thumping to something brighter, like a fire burning very dry wood.

Ruth jerked her head. Stella was standing next to her.

'Mum, listen. Hear that?'

'What? What?' Ruth sat forward in a panic. She had managed to fall asleep for a moment.

'That.' Stella nodded at Mildred's hands, still worrying at the quilt. 'That crackling.'

'Oh.' Ruth watched and listened. 'It's paper templates in the hexagons. She must have left them in when she made the quilt. People do sometimes.'

She frowned, remembering how critical her mother

35

had been of her sewing, making her unpick crooked seams and uneven stitches. 'Grandmother's Garden' was particularly trying, as one imperfectly cut hexagon could affect the whole patchwork.

'It's bothering her,' Stella announced.

'Oh, I don't think she notices things like that any longer.'

'No, it is. Look.'

Mildred was still plucking at the quilt and moaning.

'We should do something.'

Stella would choose this moment to be insistent.

'Stella, your nan has dementia, and her organs are failing. She's not thinking about the templates she left behind in a quilt!'

She had not intended to be quite so blunt. Stella stared at her, then turned and stomped out.

Ruth sighed, tears pricking the backs of her eyes. This was the sandwich-generation's plight, to be caught between dementia and adolescent strops. She considered going after her daughter, but couldn't face a full-blown argument with a teenager. Besides, the templates bothered her too. It was not like Mildred to leave papers in a patchwork quilt: it was disorderly, unfinished.

Her mother's hand flailed then and grabbed Ruth's arm, her grip surprisingly strong for a dying woman.

'Maw,' she called. 'Maw!'

She pulled her daughter's hand down to the quilt, and Ruth, with a reluctance she could not explain, ran her fingers over the patchwork rosettes. She was right:

paper templates had been left inside a cluster of flowers.

She was working out the extent of them when Stella returned with a pair of scissors and a defiant expression. Ruth flipped over a corner of the quilt.

'Cut a slit in the backing.'

Stella frowned, clearly expecting, and perhaps wanting, a fight.

'You got the scissors. Go on, then – cut it.'

Stella sliced through the quilt's green pastel backing cloth, to reveal the underside of hexagons sewn together, their quarter-inches of hem still basted around paper. Ruth froze when she spotted the templates. There were a few dozen, all made from the same lined paper covered in unfamiliar writing.

'What is that, a letter?' Stella said. 'Sick! Let's get it out.'

Mildred had normally cut up old envelopes or flyers or shopping lists for her templates; Ruth had never seen her cut up a letter. She did not want to pull out those templates. She did not want to read the hidden letter with its insistent handwriting. She wanted to take a needle and thread and sew up the slit, and, once her mother had died, burn the quilt. Ruth had always suspected that her mother's life could not have been as ordered as she made out, but she did not want to confront the potential chaos now, at the end of Mildred's days.

Stella, of course, did not feel the same way. To her it was a game, a treasure map that would reveal her grandmother's hidden chest of gold coins. Already she was pulling at the templates, ripping them in her eagerness. She was moving too fast.

'It's too hot in here,' Ruth announced. 'I'm going to get some air.'

Stella found her half an hour later on one of the benches outside the entrance. Ruth had been watching a clump of daffodils move in the breeze. She could have watched them for hours.

'Mum.' Stella sat down.

'What did it say?'

'You should read it yourself.'

'I don't want to read it. Just tell me.'

It was almost a relief to put herself into her daughter's hands.

'Nan had . . . she gave up . . . I have an auntie called Maude. I guess that's what she was trying to say when she said "Maw".'

Ruth stared at her daughter, trying to cut through the teenage tendency to turn another's news into their own personal drama.

'Mum has another daughter?'

Stella nodded. 'She wrote Nan a letter saying she'd found out she was her birth mother and could she come and see her.'

'But – when was this?'

'Like, years ago. Before I was born.'

'I have a sister. A half-sister.'

'Yeah. Oh, and there are some kids. My . . . cousins, I guess.'

Denial was flooding through her.

'Is this some kind of joke?'

'No joke. Look.'

Stella held out her phone. Even from the brief glance at the photo, Ruth could see the woman looked like Mildred, and one of her children had the same hair as Stella, down to the straggly ends.

'How did you get that?'

'It's called the Internet, Mum. She's on Facebook, and hasn't bothered with her privacy settings. I've already added her. Want to see more photos?' Stella began flicking at the screen with her thumb.

'What? No!' Ruth felt as if she were trying to stuff clothes back into a suitcase that had sprung open. This generation moved too quickly. There was no thinking, just doing. Dimly she remembered that Mildred had said something similar to her back when she was a teenager, backcombing her hair so that it stood straight up and dancing to Madness and The Jam.

'Could we just slow down for a moment, please?'

Stella regarded her with an expression that made her look ten years older.

'Mum, there's no time. You said so yourself that Nan is dying. If we want this Maude to see her, we have to contact her now.' Her phone vibrated, and she glanced at the screen.

'Look, she's confirmed me as a friend. Should I write to her? What do I say?'

She watched Stella, thumbs poised above the keys.

You have always understood my mother better than

I, Ruth thought. Maybe one day you'll give me a granddaughter who will understand me.

'Go on, then,' she said. But her daughter had already begun typing.

Snowdrop

BY JENNY COLGAN

I am watching them through the glass-panelled door of the sitting room. They are, I realise when I think about it, very outdated, these old glass panels. I should have got them changed, probably, but Geoff doesn't like spending money on things that aren't strictly necessary: 'There's nothing wrong with them,' he says, which is right, I suppose, in that they're not cracked or splotched with paint. They just look . . . tired, and they make me feel old, and I'm not. Miriam from work took the doors out of her ground floor altogether, knocked down all the walls. It's lovely. I mentioned it to Geoff, but he started talking about dust and people tramping through the house so, well, that kind of petered out. It's not that he's tight – he's lovely, but he's a bit particular about some things . . .

It's funny, the glass slightly distorts things, makes it harder to see. I've got the tea tray stabilised against the door: I really need someone to open it for me, but they look so deep in conversation. I can't hear what they're saying, but David's mouth is open and Geoff is gesticulating at him. Through the blur – I am constantly furious that I'm old enough to need glasses. Truly spitting about it. I'm sure I lose them so often as a form of subconscious protest.

Anyway, I've left my dratted glasses in the kitchen, and David and Geoff look so alike it's ridiculous, both of them with slightly bad posture. David much thinner, of course, but Geoff just sniffs at that and says, 'Just you wait, all that rubbish you eat,' and David sighs and rolls his eyes because he is twenty, and so knows everything.

I wish they wouldn't give each other such a hard time, like they're from different planets. Geoff's not even fifty. He's perfectly normal, except when David is in the room, then they both start to bristle. I don't know what it is now, David turned up out of the blue. Not like him on a Sunday morning: normally we have to wait for him to come back from college. I know some kids come back all the time, every week, but Geoff and I agreed that's not at all healthy, they need to cut the apron strings, and Geoff occasionally mutters that, 'If David thinks he's coming back here to sit on his arse once he's finished his course, he's got another think coming,' which makes him sound like his own dad. Although that's the good thing about Geoff not liking to spend money around the house. David's bedroom is still there, just as he left it. Obviously I never find myself in there, like some daft middle-aged woman. I have work and Zumba and loads of things to do. Loads.

I head back to the kitchen. There is some old dirty

snow on the ground, with a snowdrop pushing its way out of it. I love snowdrops, they're such stupid flowers. Keep on pushing and pushing to be beautiful, even when it's freezing and miserable. I know this seems daft, but it's almost like they do it just to cheer us up when we're in the dumps.

Geoff seems to be shouting now. Oh God, what is it? For the last few years they've spoken about nothing but football, really, because it's safe ground. Not politics, of course, not the town – David thinks we're all really naff and stupid around here, horribly provincial, which is his way of talking about the nice house in the lovely safe village we took out a huge mortgage to buy because we wanted to give him somewhere idyllic to grow up, away from smoky cities full of traffic and muggers. So of course he hates it, went hurtling off to Leeds first chance he got.

Then last year the football team started losing – not just losing like they normally did, but really losing – and they managed to fall out over that too, blaming tactics or management or 'lazy, spoilt players who think the world owes them a living, like you', Geoff had said, never quite getting over his disappointment at David doing Media Studies at university and not something that would end up with a job, not these days. David doesn't know how much his dad worries about how much tougher things are these days than when we were starting out. Sometimes I wonder if I think of the nineties as idyllic because we were a young

43

family and it was lovely. Sometimes I think they really were.

Geoff's never said it out loud, but he'd have loved another engineer in the family. David has said it out loud about a million times, he'd rather die than do what his dad does, and Geoff points out that it fed and clothed him, and David rolls his eyes and that really sets Geoff off again.

He's brought Ellie. To be honest, she's the kind of girl that slightly frightens me. I know that's ridiculous, I'm forty-eight, and in pretty good shape, and far too old to be intimidated by anyone any more, surely.

But I can't remember ever being this confident in my late teens; I don't think any of us were. She's so well groomed – her nails and hair are always perfect, a big blonde mane down her back. She's not tarty-looking, just confident and sure of herself and polite, but in a slightly knowing way I can't quite put my finger on, so that when she says, 'Oh, wow, all your saucers and cups match!' I can't tell if she's slightly making fun of me or not. It annoys me, too; I'm just a person, we could just have a normal conversation without her having to comment on how tidy the house is all the time. Geoff says David lives in a pigsty. I guess that's probably why he doesn't ask us up to Leeds, and Geoff wouldn't like to waste money on hotels anyway.

Sometimes I see large families out with teenagers; yelling, talking noisily, laughing, sharing a glass of wine together like they're friends. Miriam's daughter comes over to the office for lunch quite a lot. Lunch! In the week! She only works round the corner, didn't even want to go away to college. At the time Miriam was disappointed, and I was so proud of David, but now I'm not so sure. She's a lovely girl, Laurel.

Oh goodness, they are fighting. I'll wait in the kitchen till it's all over. It will be the same old thing, I know. Stupid stags butting antlers in the woods.

It was so soft, the warmth in the air, so gentle, the colours of the sea and the sky weren't strong at all, out of season; in the evening the water went pink and purple and violet and the scent of the bougainvillea, and the warm rocks it grew between, descended, and we had found a little place just right out on the sand – just tables and chairs, really, strewn on the beach, I can't even imagine you'd be allowed to do that now – and we had explained early on how much lire we had (hardly any at all), and the man had smiled and said, 'Well, you come to us and eat what we eat,' and we went every night and ate what they fed the kitchen staff, no menus, nothing.

But oh, what did we eat? Great big stews with tentacles and who knew what sticking out of them; great, thick, heavy, fishy broths. Geoff and me, who'd grown up on mince and potatoes and eating what you were given and apple crumble with Carnation Milk. We ate scallops, and something which, over much laughter, we finally realised was boar; and tiny little fried fish and great huge plates of oily, slick pasta covered in black olives – we didn't even know what they were – and there was a great big chipped jug filled with fruity red wine the same temperature as the sea that never seemed to empty.

And we held hands and sometimes the chef and the waiter and the pot-washer would join us and try out their few words of English, and we would attempt a little Italian, but mostly it was just us and our tent on top of the cliff, which we would climb up unsteadily every night, partly from the wine, partly because we were so dazzled by the shocking brightness of the stars and the warmth of that air. I had rarely been out in the dark without a cardigan before.

So we thought it was that, of course, eating from a kitchen they wouldn't send a health inspector to in a million years, when I couldn't stop throwing up. Then they found a doctor; so handsome, and we had to pay him, we didn't realise, it was so embarrassing watching a doctor standing there and taking money. After he'd examined me and asked me questions in broken English, and Geoff stood there, fumbling with his wallet, me slightly panicking as he handed over the last of our lire – our credit-card limit was about fifty quid then, I think – he turned to me and I thought, Oh, he's going to be so cross about the money. I knew what he was like even then; but he was beaming, he was just beaming. And that's how we knew David was coming.

People say it goes fast, children growing up. They don't say how awful it is; every time they grow out of their shoes, or change schools, or stop saying 'mine' when they mean 'my', and you realise that that is gone now, that that child has disappeared and there is another in his place. Your world becomes full of last things, of endings.

We never had more; Geoff worried about the money, but David also – he was our world. He was absolutely enough, I always felt. His smell, his little ears, his funny sayings, the way he fitted his hands in between our hands so we could swing him always when he walked. Who could want more than this? Except he kept growing, of course, and he no longer wanted to hold hands, then cuddle on the sofa, then kiss us goodnight, then, it felt, have anything to do with us at all.

And for a while after that I felt so, so cheated. Why hadn't I had dozens? Loads? Every time one was out of nappies I should have just had another. We'd have got by. And I nearly had time, I nearly did, I was only in my early forties. People did, all the time. Not us, though. We were too late. I mean, I like work, but it's not my great career, my great interest. I was always just so interested in David. He was – is – so uninterested in me. The curl of the hand in mine, the gentle, trusting expression, the endless questions. All of it gone.

Him and his nice, awkward dad, so alike, spending all of Saturday afternoon in the shed, in almost complete silence, then calling me in, both of them ecstatic, to see the model Concorde they had completed at last, perfectly painted. And David said, 'Could we go on Concorde, Dad?' and Geoff said, 'Son, if I had the money, we would,' which I, for once, believed, but then, one morning, without telling me, Geoff woke David very early and they both snuck out and found a place on the perimeter of Heathrow – you could do that in those days – to watch her take off.

He never remembers that, David. He is selfish, of course. He's allowed; he's young. He thinks we're all idiots. Does Geoff remember, I wonder?

OK, I have my stupid ugly specs on now. My brave snowdrop is waving itself in the horrid winter wind. I am ready. Maybe a cup of tea and a biscuit will help settle things down. It's meant to, isn't it?

I push open the door. It's gone silent. David is bright red. Ellie is staring at the floor. Geoff is gazing out of the window in disbelief.

'Hello!' I say, as brightly as I can. 'How nice to see you all.'

Geoff turns to me, his face handsome, still, to me, and I know, just in the split second before he tells me; suddenly I realise.

'He's only knocked up a lass,' he says. Ellie doesn't even look up.

I quietly place the tea tray on the occasional table.

'Well that,' I say, 'is wonderful news.'

And I mean it. Their faces, all of them surprised, look up at me. And they know that I do.

Now I feel like perhaps we can all get started.

Sacrifices

BY R. J. ELLORY

*S*acrifices had to be made.

That was the nature of life, the business of being human. Significant, insignificant, they were made constantly. Sacrifices of time, of energy, of effort, of attention.

Kathleen Reynolds, Fairfax County Homicide Division, had let go of everything for her career. No husband, no kids, no Thanksgiving Dinner with a horde of Reynoldses crowding the table with laughter and love. No Christmas. No birthdays.

There had been relationships, of course – brief, physical, almost perfunctory, and always with other cops, because cops seemed to be the only people in the world who could understand who she was, why she had chosen this road.

Kathleen had two cell phones, one for her personal life, one for work. The personal one never rang. The work one rang constantly, and every time it rang there was a dead person at the end. A twelve-year-old in pieces in a dumpster back of the Carlton Grand on West Seventh and Houston; a gangland assassination;

a betrayed wife who'd finally, finally, finally had enough and put a boning knife through her lying, cheating, two-faced husband's heart. And while Kathleen was there, stationed at the crime scene, up to her proverbial neck in the remnants of someone's life, she could get another call, and yet another.

Come from this side of the city, she was investigating your homicide alongside five or six others; come from the other side of the city and your death was being investigated by her and half a dozen additional cops. Life was not fair, never had been, never would be. Perhaps it was never meant to be that way. A sentiment came to mind whenever she was faced with such a situation, a sentiment echoed by the county fire chief, a man she knew in more ways than one. 'Ain't never put out a fire in a rich white guy's house,' he told Kathleen. 'Seems to me I'm only ever dealing with those who have everything to lose, and then just go right ahead and lose it.'

She'd seen things that had aged her a year in an afternoon. Or she would be gone for a week, a temporary reassignment, perhaps, and return to find her colleagues had aged by a decade.

This was the job. The brightest and the best wrestling forever with the darkest and the worst. But what else was there to do? This was her calling, her vocation, her life. This belief in what she was doing, this sense of duty, was the thing for which all the sacrifices had been made.

Sometimes you came to the conclusion that the only

thing you didn't have enough time for was to make changes.

Bitsy stood at the door to the bedroom.

She could hear the sound of her mother's faltering breathing. It had worsened, just in a matter of hours it had worsened, and with each straining inhalation, Bitsy felt as if a hand was once again twisting her heart.

It seemed to Bitsy that you could always run out of things to laugh about, but things that made you cry? Hell, they just seemed to keep on coming.

Bitsy's eyes carried a weight of sadness, a burden of grief. Here was a woman who not only remembered the past, she longed to live there. A past where her mother was well, where her father was still alive, where the world had some sense of balance, some sense of order.

Now it was all crazy. Now none of it made sense. Now the things she had believed in for so long just seemed to be so fragile, so empty, just pulling apart at the seams.

Sometimes she felt that all the madness the world could muster was rushing headlong toward her.

Seemed to Bitsy that we all made a deal with God. If we believed, if we trusted, then everything would be fine. But it wasn't fine. Never had been, probably never would be. Seemed to her that someone somewhere wasn't holding up their end of the deal.

She hesitated a moment longer, and then she crossed the room to the edge of the bed. She didn't even know whether her mother would recognise her any more.

Bitsy looked at the drip, the line that carried the morphine, and she just nudged the release valve a millimeter to the right.

Her mother's breathing seemed to ease, or was that Bitsy's imagination? The morphine helped with the pain, of course, but it didn't slow or inhibit the virulent aggression of the cancer that had taken her mother from her by degrees.

Her mother was dissolving, disappearing; being slowly, painfully erased from the face of the earth.

There was nothing right about this. She could not understand, appreciate, reconcile, accept; even in the quieter moments when she managed to snatch an hour's agitated rest, she would wake to the certainty that it was all a dream.

What would her father have said? He would have been forthright, brave, calm, almost wordless, perhaps a pillar of strength; perhaps, in truth, incapable of showing any real emotion.

Bitsy did not know what he would have said.

And now it did not matter.

Kathleen Reynolds knew that everyone was some mother's child. Didn't matter who they were, where they came from, how they got here or what they did when they arrived – they were still some mother's child.

Life was life. No one had the right to deny the life of

another. Death was unconditional. Death accepted everyone. In death there was no racism, no bigotry, no intolerance, no division, no separation of race, color, creed, age or gender. Death would just as easily take a five-year-old girl who had seen no life at all, as it would a sixty-year-old serial killer who had committed the worst atrocities imaginable. It was what we all had in common: being born, and dying.

In all her years of police-department service, she had drawn her gun twenty, maybe thirty times. She had fired it ten or twelve times, no more, and never directly to end a life. Always a warning shot, then the leg, the shoulder, and she was grateful that she had never encountered a situation where that fatal decision had to be made.

There were officers who had, and from that point forward, you knew something was broken inside.

The law was the law. If there was no law, there was no order, and without order there was chaos, anarchy, war. Society could not survive without law, and regardless of rights or wrongs, regardless of ethics, morals or justice, the law was still the law.

To Serve and Protect. That's why she was a police officer. That's why she had made such sacrifices.

That was the reason for her existence.

Bitsy sat quietly for a while. She was tired, always so tired.

She knew she had to do this thing. Now there was no doubt in her mind. There would be consequences.

Always there were consequences. Life as she knew it would be over, not only for her mother but for herself as well.

You can allow someone to die, or you can help them.

Such things were far from one another. They were different countries, different worlds.

She tried to imagine what her father would say, and again could not.

This was not selfish; it was selfless. This was not cruel, it was merciful. This would not be killing her mother, it would be releasing her.

But there were still consequences.

The police would be involved, of course. They would want to question her, to try to understand why she had done this thing, her rationale, her motive, her intent. She would go to court, and some tough detective would stand in the dock and tell the world what had happened. There would be a psych examination, some half-hearted attempt by state-assigned defenders to isolate the underlying mental and emotional stresses that had driven her to this. Perhaps they would cite her job as a contributory factor. Perhaps those prosecutors would identify the thin threads of despair and frustration and hopelessness, and somehow they would weave them into a rope strong enough to hang her. Or not.

She did not know.

She did not care.

Whatever strength she possessed, it was insufficient to see her mother suffer any longer.

*

In Kathleen Reynolds's mind, if serving and protecting meant taking care of those who did not deserve such care, or those who were guilty, freed by some technicality that excused their garbage cans from the search warrant, then so be it. That was the nature of things, and until some bleeding-heart liberal do-gooder arrived with some better, more effective solution, then these were the lines within which they had to walk. We – as people – had created this system, and we – as people – had to use it, maintain it, support it, allow it to evolve and grow with us. Otherwise, what? Otherwise there was nothing.

If there was one thing Kathleen Reynolds knew about, it was the creativity and imagination that could be employed to bring a life to an end. She also knew how it was to spend your working hours reviled and rejected and despised by people: people who didn't know you, would never know you, not until something happened, not until the world delivered one of its unmentionable horrors to their door. And then you became everything and everyone. Then you became the most important person in the world – friend, confidante, confessor, vigilante.

Everyone wanted justice. Everyone wanted to see the guilty brought to book until it was they themselves who were guilty, and then they pleaded for all manner of mercies, quoting phrases from TV shows, talking about human rights, questioning evidence, the veracity of identification, fingerprints, eyewitness accounts, bystander statements.

But guilt was guilt, and innocence was innocence. One could not be twisted to look like the other, and even if some vague approximation was made, the guilty still knew it.

What you did was what you did, and you abided by the law, or you paid the price.

Didn't matter the circumstances, the explanation, the justification, the provocation.

The world was hard. It was sharp corners and rough edges. The world forgot, but it did not forgive.

She remembered her first partner, a hard-faced and bitter veteran. He'd shook her hand roughly, slapped her on the shoulder and started their first day together with, 'Well hell, lady, let's get you out there and see if we can't get you stabbed or shot, eh?'

She had been stabbed. She had been shot at. She had survived. But for what? For a principle, a belief, a faith in something so fragile, so tenuous? Seemed so. Seemed that was just the way of things.

Bitsy knew it was time.

She'd sat there for a seeming eternity, her eyes closed, but still the salt sting of tears behind her lids. Her throat was a Gordian knot of tense muscle. She knew she would never be able to swallow again.

She opened her eyes slowly, saw her own hands on the arms of the chair, the bloodless knuckles, the way the veins stood up from her wrists.

This was it.

The time had come.

She rose slowly, her weight twice, three times what she remembered, and each step toward the bed was laborious, almost painful.

Nothing compared to the pain her mother had endured, was still enduring – and that was why this had to be done.

She stood there at the end of the mattress. She remembered all the hours, the days, the weeks, the months she had stood right there willing her mother back to health, back to life, willing it with every ounce of anything she could muster – and she had failed.

In this now, this final act of mercy, she could not fail.

She pictured her father's face. Why could she never imagine what he would say? Had she known so little of him? Had he been a complete stranger to her?

Bitsy raised her hand.

Her fingers touched the valve, and slowly, millimeter by millimeter, she released it.

Again, was it her imagination, or could she hear the morphine as it made its way along the narrow plastic tube toward her mother's arm?

She could go back now. Right now. She could pull that needle right out of her mother before the morphine reached her.

But no, she did not.

She stood there, listening to nothing but the faltering sound of her mother's breathing, the sound of her own breathing in her tight and frightened chest, feeling the weight of her heart as it tried to pump her murderous blood through her arteries, her pulse as it insisted in her temples – *killer . . . killer . . . killer . . .*

For that's what she was now: a killer.

There would be consequences.

Bitsy leaned forward. She touched her hand to her mother's cheek, and then she kissed her forehead.

'Goodbye Mom,' she whispered. 'When you find Dad, tell him I'm sorry, that I always loved him . . . Tell him that he was always so much hard work. Tell him I tried my best, tried to follow in his footsteps, but those footsteps were too big . . .'

Her voice cracked. She tried to swallow, but she could not.

Her mother seemed to open her eyes, but Bitsy knew this was purely her imagination.

She tried to see her mother smile. She tried so hard.

Bitsy knew then. She knew as well as she knew her own name.

Her mother was gone.

Bitsy closed the door gently behind her. She made her way down the hall and picked up the telephone. She dialed the police.

'I am calling to report a murder,' she said, and then she gave her name, her address. 'I've killed my mother,' she told them. 'I killed her with morphine.'

She was surprised at how many questions they asked her, but she knew that the operator was keeping her on the line, letting her talk, keeping her engaged so she wouldn't run in some last desperate moment of panic. A squad car was on the way. Bitsy knew that.

'Don't worry,' she told the operator. 'I'm not going to run. I'm not going anywhere. I'll be right here when they arrive. I am ready to accept the consequences for what I have done.' And then she hung up the phone and went back to her mother's room.

Bitsy was surprised to see who appeared in the doorway eight minutes later.

'Frank?' she said.

Frank nodded.

'She's dead, Frank,' Bitsy said.

'I know,' said Frank. 'They told me what happened, and I didn't want anyone to come here but me.'

Frank walked to the foot of the bed. He looked down at Bitsy's mother.

'I'm not going to ask why,' he said. 'I know how much you have been through.'

Bitsy stood up. She held out her hands. 'You want to cuff me?'

Frank smiled. 'I don't think that will be necessary.'

They walked to the door together.

Bitsy paused, glanced back, hesitated.

'What is it?' Frank asked.

'All this time I've been thinking about my father,' she said. 'Trying to imagine what he would do, what he would say. He was such a tough guy, such a man's man, and I couldn't imagine what he would say.'

She shook her head. 'I know what he would say now.'

Frank said nothing, and waited for Bitsy to go on.

'He would tell me I had done what I believed was right, and that was more important than anything else.'

Bitsy looked at Frank, and she smiled.

' "Bitsy," ' he would say, "you did what you felt was right, and I am proud of you for that." '

Frank frowned. 'Bitsy?' he asked.

'That's what he called me,' Kathleen said. 'That's what Dad used to call me as a baby. I was so tiny. Itsy-Bitsy, he'd call me, and he never called me anything else.'

Kathleen Reynolds closed her eyes for just a second, and then she led the way to her own front door and never looked back.

Aphrodite's Rock

BY JULIA GREGSON

Cyprus, 1953

On the day after the memorial service, Lorna woke feeling perfectly – and not unpleasantly – blank, almost like a dead thing herself. The RAF Benevolent Fund had flown her here, putting her up in an empty house at a place called Paramali in the Limassol district of Cyprus. It was the usual kind of Married Quarters house, with other people's left-behind furniture in the sitting room, their safety pins in the bedroom drawers, but this one had orange trees in the garden and a veranda, a staggering view of the turquoise sea and the clearest, bluest skies she'd ever seen. She and Tom had flown here in a rattling and noisy Beverley, her first and, she hoped, last trip in an aeroplane. Tom had been thrilled by it: the sick bags, the cardboard box with sandwiches under the seat, the plastic knife and fork, the chocolate.

The morning light was blinding. She closed her eyes, lay back on her pillow and, hearing the unsteady

Julia Gregson

rattle of a tea tray on the stairs, suddenly yelled, 'Oh darling, be careful, you really . . .'

'Silence mother.' Tom, who was ten, opened the door with his foot. He put the tray down on the bed, concentrating fiercely.

'Me heap good at this,' he said in his Indian-chief voice. He scowled under his fringe, so like Ned it hurt.

'Bread.' He clumped down two inexpertly hacked slices of the Greek bread they'd found in the market.

'Honey.' He'd left the spoon in the jar.

'A bit of butter.' (A bit! Half a week's ration at least, if they'd been in England.)

'Flowers.' He put a jam jar on the bedside table with two passion flowers in it.

They'd found the passion flowers yesterday, scrambling up a trellis on the side of the veranda. She was showing Tom the delicate tendrils of the purple crown of thorns, the twelve petals and sepals for the apostles, the little green hammer for the holy lance when he sighed and moved away from her, and ran around the lawn making aeroplane sounds.

Today, he took one of the passion flowers from the jam jar and examined it forensically.

'They are awfully funny-looking, aren't they?' he said, holding it right up to his eye. 'They look as if they're trying to be sick.'

When the tea shot through her nose, he began to laugh too, throwing himself extravagantly about the bed, glad to have made her happy, and relieved too, she imagined.

62

Yesterday, he'd made everything worse by appearing in her room at six in the morning, pale as death, saying he'd changed his mind about laying the wreath.

'I didn't even know him,' he'd shouted when she'd insisted.

'I'm sorry,' she'd apologised to Jack when he came to pick them up in the car. Jack was Squadron Leader Thompson, who'd been posted to Cyprus after the war. He'd been assigned to look after them because he was a friend of Ned's before the war.

'But he's adamant, and I'm not sure what to do.'

'Leave him,' he'd said. 'He'll come.'

And he had; dashing from the house at the very last minute, red-faced and sweating in his school suit, his hair slicked down with water.

On the farm where she'd spent her childhood, she'd seen it happen: how the sweetest of foals grew in the wink of an eye into bargy, unmanageable stallions, all eyes, teeth and heels. You had to stand up to them.

'Now look at me, Tom, and listen,' she said later over the washing-up. 'I know yesterday was hard and horrible, and I know you were upset, but you were rude to Jack, and to me, and you must behave better today. Got it? Good. End of lecture.'

They gazed at each other warily; tears swelled at the edges of Tom's eyes. He hated crying in front of her; in his mind he was her protector.

'I didn't know him,' he said through unsteady lips. 'I was only saying the truth.'

Well, grief was an untidy thing. She knew that now.

Yesterday, after the ceremony and the drink in the Officers' Mess, Jack had taken them out for a picnic. She liked Jack. He was tall and blond with an aquiline nose and clever, questing eyes: a reader, a thinker, the sort of man who under normal circumstances she might have found attractive.

She'd met, but not exactly clocked him, twelve years ago when he and Ned were at flying school at Bracknell, a time when she and Ned were so blindly besotted, all they could think about was each other and sneaking off to talk in cheap cafés, or to some friend's room where they could make love.

But yesterday, during the dreaded ceremony, it was a uniformed Jack who stood solidly beside her. She'd watched the formal gestures of grief through what felt like a pane of glass: the laying of the wreath, the business with the ceremonial swords, and later, the tense drinks party in the dazzlingly bright Officers' Club, where people who'd never even met Ned pressed her hand sympathetically and said what rotten bad luck it had been, he sounded like a splendid chap. When one stranger, sincere, maybe sloshed, had mentioned the cruel timing of it happening two days after the war had ended, the pane of glass slipped and she remembered the flat again, wearing the blue dress Ned loved, laying out cutlery for their first meal, hardly able to breathe with excitement at the thought of telling him they were going to have a baby.

'Sorry I was rude, Mummy,' Tom intoned, eyes down. 'But Jack was quite boring yesterday.'

'He was trying to cheer us up, you little savage, and he was interesting – I love hearing about the history here.'

'Well, you like culture and things,' Tom mumbled. 'I don't.'

After the memorial service, Jack had taken them in his dusty Renault to see the sights: the Paphos Lighthouse, where he told Tom about the Phoenician sailors and their gold and trinkets, the Romans, the pirates beating their boats against the rocks. He'd driven them along the coast to see Aphrodite's Rock.

She'd been sitting beside him looking at the sea when a wave of grief and something like anger swept over her: the sense of everything that would now never happen. No sunlit days with Ned; no mornings in bed; no getting to know him again; and, worst of all, he would never, ever meet this boy of theirs.

Jack unpacked a bottle of wine and some sandwiches, Men's sandwiches, she thought detachedly, seeing the hunks of bread and cheese, the few olives stuffed in an envelope. He'd broken the silence by saying that Aphrodite's Rock was famous.

'How can a rock be famous?' Tom scowled. He threw a stone into the sea.

'Manners, Tom!' she said. 'Jack was only trying to be nice.'

'I'm sorry,' she said to Jack. They had watched her son's skinny frame stride into the water. 'You probably think we should be over it by now.'

She'd wiped her eyes surreptitiously on the sandwich wrapper.

He put his hand on her wrist.

'He was my best friend,' he said. 'I thought about leaving the Air Force when they posted me back here.'

She looked at him properly for the first time. 'Why didn't you?'

'Because—'

A yell interrupted them. Tom was standing at the top of the rock. He was teetering on the edge. He was waving. 'Look at meeeee.'

She saw him leap through the dazzling air, the water exploding in diamonds around him, a dive-bomb that made a sound like a cannon exploding.

'I like your boy,' Jack said. 'He's a trickful bouncer.'

After her breakfast in bed, Tom swam all morning and then they had lunch on the veranda: their first melon ever, tasting of flowers and honey, then scrambled eggs for him – bright yellow eggs from local hens.

'So, will Mummy be swimming today?' Tom teased. Her new swimsuit, with its brave little diver embroidered on its skirt, was still in the suitcase.

'Be Afroflighty, or whatever her name was.'

And she'd imagined the goddess, vigorous and sunlit, bursting in a plume of spray from the sea. When she'd asked Jack yesterday to tell her the legend, partly to make up for Tom's rudeness, he'd said, 'Oh! Later, maybe.'

I've made him look wary, she'd thought, and regretted it.

'I'd like to know,' she'd said.

'Well . . . the legend is that if a woman swims around the rock, she'll be fertile for ever.'

And she'd gone beetroot red, which was annoying.

In the cicada-loud afternoon, she sat on a cane chair on the veranda, basking in the heat like a cat. Tom was inside reading the *Beano*.

'I'm definitely going to swim later today,' she was shouting when her voice was drowned out by the roar of a motorbike reaching a shrill and unpleasant crescendo on the other side of the veranda. She shaded her eyes, frowning, and when she opened the gate, there was Jack, in goggles, riding a motorbike with a sidecar attached.

Jack brought the bike to a skidding show-off halt.

'I thought we should have an adventure,' he said.

Tom jumped off the sofa. He punched the air with both fists. 'Dambusters,' he shouted pointlessly, his new word for all good things. 'It's a flying machine.'

He crashed upstairs, shouting, 'Give me a sec to get my goggles.'

'You didn't say you were bringing this,' she said to Jack.

'Should I have warned you?' he said.

'Maybe.' Her mouth stiffened.

'Boys like dangerous things,' he said.

'You don't say,' she said quietly and bitterly. They stared at each other.

'Is it safe?'

'Yep.' He was grinning at her – a lean, fit young pilot today, in his dusty clothes and desert boots.

'It's the best way to see this island. Hop on.'

'You there.' Jack unlatched the sidecar door; Tom did a flying leap inside.

'You behind me,' he said to her, and revved the engine. 'I won't bite. Promise.'

She stepped on, gingerly, at first holding the fabric of his shirt. When the start flung her against him, she put her arms around his waist in a neutral sort of way as if he were, say, a post.

Tom, strapped in the sidecar, looked up, beaming. The happiest she'd seen him for ages.

'Hurt him,' she swore into Jack's back, 'and I'll ruddy well kill you.'

Jack drove fast and well up to the top of the cliff to show them the best views of the sea, then down to the stables in the valley where Arab horses with coats like new pennies were being groomed, and where Tom was taught how to give one an apple, flattening his hands to avoid its terrifying teeth.

This calmed her: she liked horses and felt at home with them. She was patting a sweet-faced mare when she looked up and saw the tiny figure of her son riding the motorbike down the dusty path that led from the stables and into a grove of olive trees. He was sitting in front of Jack, the bike ricocheting wildly from side to side as it shrieked and roared into the trees, leaving dust and birds in the air.

'Stupid, stupid, stupid!' she raged as she ran down the path. She would hit him when she saw him, she would sodding well kill him. He had pretended to be gentle and understanding, and done this crazy thing.

She was wet with sweat; she could hear her own hoarse panting as she imagined Tom's face, all smashed, his fractured limbs, the horror all over again.

She ran to a bend in the path, saw the glint of a pond beyond, and turning the corner she saw Tom's blue shirt and both of them lying in the dust in a hollow of earth near some stunted carob trees. 'I knew it,' she grieved, seeing buzzards flying above them. 'I knew it.'

It took a while to see they were laughing. Tom stood up, squeaking and with tears running down his face, and then he ran around her in a lap of honour with his arms stretched out.

'I did it, Mum. All by myself.' He punched Jack lightly on the arm and kept on running.

'You bastard,' she said.

Jack looked at her. 'I was steering,' he told her quietly. 'I had my hand on the accelerator. All under control.'

Tom, still running, shouted, 'Let's go swimming before lunch.'

They ate supper together in a Turkish restaurant overlooking Paphos harbour: fish caught that day, washed down with several glasses of retsina, Coca-Cola for Tom. She felt sun-filled, hollow-legged, worn out by swimming and that day's terrors. Her hair felt stiff with salt – she didn't care.

When it grew dark and the moon came out, they swam in water warm as milk, so Tom could see the phosphorescence. The boy stared and stared at the tiny lapidary explosions of light under the water, and she, doing her not-very-efficient doggy paddle, was thinking, When I get back home, I shall clear out Ned's wardrobe. That I can do.

Earlier, over coffee at the restaurant, Jack had said, in the simplest and most general way possible, that he was thirty-six years old now, that it was days like this that made him see how much he wanted children. Well, maybe it was a hint, or maybe a promise; she was in no mood to analyse or plan anything, but simply to enjoy this moment under bright stars and in warm water, watching the pinpricks of light glow and go out again.

Divorced

BY TESSA HADLEY

*F*rank stopped off at his daughter's new flat on his way home from work. He had a key because he had been supporting Gemma through her move from London, checking the landlord had fixed what he'd promised he'd fix, helping her unpack and put up shelves. When he let himself in the door, he thought the place would be empty (Gemma had a job interview, and afterwards was meeting an old friend for a drink). The flat was on the first floor of a big Edwardian house, on a street that Frank reassured himself was all right – scruffy, but not dodgy; better than some of the places she had lived in London. Gemma was thirty, she'd split up with the idiot who'd been her boyfriend for ten years; heartbroken, she'd decided to come home to the city where she'd grown up. Frank had always wanted her to come home, but he still couldn't forgive the idiot.

Stepping inside the flat, he saw that a woman was washing up at the sink in the kitchen, with her back to him. It wasn't Gemma, who was plump and small and young; this woman was tall, with a fuzz of grey hair that stood out round her head against the light. The conversion had been done with the kitchen at the front, in the bay window, partitioned off from the rest of the living room by a peninsula of kitchen units. 'It'll be nice for you, cooking in the sunshine,' Frank had suggested hopefully when they first looked round. Gemma had glared at him; who did she have to cook for now? (Even when she was nine years old – or five, or three – she had had this gift of making him feel as if he'd put his clumsy foot on her fine sensitivities.)

The stranger was calmly rinsing a plate under the tap. A cardboard box, the same as the boxes piled up all over the floor, was open on the draining board; she must be unpacking Gemma's china and washing it. She wasn't dressed for washing up; a navy jacket with a white trim was hung across the back of a chair, the sleeves of her white shirt were rolled to the elbows and a watch and gold charm bracelet and a jumble of rings were set aside on the counter. 'Hello, Frank,' she said, in a familiar creaky, aching, smoky voice. 'Long time no see.'

Of course – it was Hazel. As soon as he knew it he thought he must have known it all along.

Hazel was Gemma's mother, Frank's ex-wife. They'd been exes since Gemma was ten, but naturally through her teenage years they'd seen each other often, mostly through a haze of hostility. Since Gemma moved to London they'd not had any reason to meet, though they'd talked a few times about practicalities on the phone. They hadn't bumped into one another, or not for years – surprisingly, in this modestly sized city. Frank supposed their spheres didn't intersect. He had a business chemically cleaning industrial plants, which didn't make him rich and sometimes hardly made him any money. And Hazel – whose news he always heard, sooner or later, through Gemma – was a senior manager at the hospital.

Both Frank and Hazel were happy in new relationships (Gemma, long-suffering in their conflict, had carried that news, too, between them). So there was no explanation for the lift of excitement Frank felt when he saw Hazel at the sink, washing their daughter's dishes. He hadn't thought of this aspect of Gemma's return, that his path was bound to cross with her mother's again. When Hazel turned round, he saw that she looked startlingly older, but also softer: wearing less make-up, her expression not guarded with the old ferocity. Skinny women like Hazel didn't age well; gravity was blurring the eyes and cheeks, which had been so hard and clear, dragging them down. But then, when Hazel was beautiful, twelve or fifteen years ago, Frank had more or less hated her (her wolfish, lean jaw, lashes black as spilled ink, swelling lower lip, fine-cartilaged long nose). For a few moments, his ex-wife's past face and her present hovered separately in Frank's perception before he adjusted to the difference. And no doubt Hazel was staring at him too, making the same adjustments – with less reason to be impressed. When it came to his looks, he'd lost just about everything except weight; he'd certainly lost whatever style he used to have. Luckily, she was smiling at him as if style didn't count for as much with her as it used to. She dried her hands on a tea towel.

'Gem texted me,' she said, screwing her rings back on her fingers one by one, in a gesture he knew as intimately as if it was his own. 'She didn't get the job.'

Frank had his own opinion about that job – it was the same one Gemma had had before she left for London ten years ago, serving in a dress shop, way below her abilities. He would have come out with his opinion forcefully, but Hazel's presence, so surprisingly familiar and unfamiliar, constrained him: he only said it was a shame.

Over the next weeks and months, Frank and Hazel saw a lot of one another. Gemma was in a bad way; she needed them. First, she couldn't get a job, then she got a job that she didn't like, as a receptionist at an orthodontist's, and all the time she was still heartbroken over that idiot, Joey. Hazel laughed at Frank's calling him an idiot; she seemed to have more time for him, she even suggested that Gemma might be quite a handful in a relationship. Loyally, Frank refused to contemplate it.

'Come on, Frank,' said Hazel. 'Remember all the things about me that used to drive you mad? Times that by ten.'

It was evening and they had struggled together, setting up Gemma's computer; Gemma was out at another of those sessions with her old girlfriends in the wine bar from which she returned drunk and indignant, with puffy eyes. Frank tried to remember exactly what it was about Hazel that had driven him mad. He had always presumed that the past stayed behind him in its place, like an illustrated calendar of days and hours that he could dip into if he wanted, if only he ever had the time. Reaching back, he found that the sequences of past everyday experiences were crumbled to a few fragments; there were pictures, but there was nothing much behind the pictures. What had Hazel actually said and done, that he hadn't been able to forgive? He had been so sure, at the time, that he'd known what she was like, and that what she was like was awful. He remembered her getting dressed up once when they were going out somewhere, in a tearing hurry as usual, leaning into the mirror to hook the earrings into her pierced lobes, the eyes in her reflection meeting his real ones, skidding off them again in impatience. She had seemed to see right through him then, or right into him, and not to be pleased with what she saw; and he had seemed, too, to look down into the depths of her, where something was toxic and ruthless and she was fixed on having her own way. The very things about her he was most attracted to – her leggy stride, her leather jacket, her crinkling auburn hair worn long and loose – had appeared in those days as emanations of her willpower, turned against him.

But that was then.

They got online eventually, and while Frank search-ed the Internet for new jobs for Gemma, Hazel filled two glasses from a bottle of Prosecco she'd bought. She studied him frowning at the screen. 'Thirty years old,' she said, 'and you're still babying her. No wonder she's such a mess.'

This was a battle cry from their old time; but Frank didn't take offence. (Perhaps Hazel was right, perhaps he had spoilt his daughter because he was so afraid of hurting her. Gemma ought to be standing on her own two feet by now.) She didn't seem to mean to offend him, either; he only amused her. Nothing, it seemed, could start up the fight again between him and his ex-wife. He teased her that his taxes went to pay for her good public-sector pension, but she didn't rise to his bait. 'You'll be glad enough of the National Health when you need it,' she said – and it was true, he had recently had to cancel his private health insurance because his company was feeling the recession.

Giving up on his Internet search, he chinked glasses with her and they sat waiting together for their daughter. Outside in the street the wind raked through the trees, blew rain against the windowpane. They both had homes to go to – warm, tidy, comfortable homes; Frank had widescreen TV and a big L-shaped leather sofa. But they seemed to like lingering in this flat that felt as provisional as a camp in the wilderness, among the boxes Gemma still hadn't finished unpacking; the walls were dotted with nails and little dust marks where the previous tenant had hung his pictures. They talked about everything. In Frank's relationship with Julia (he'd been with her for nearly twenty years), it was Julia who talked. He didn't mind this; he was famous for being a bear who growled and retreated behind his newspaper, or to his computer. That was supposed to be his character. But he and Hazel had known one another when they were very young and their characters weren't fixed, and now they were at ease like comrades who'd fought together in an old war. He told her his plans, how he wanted to sell the business and buy a boat and set off in it for a year.

'You'll hate it,' said Hazel. 'It's one of your mistakes. You get an idea that something will suit you and you rush into it, then you find that the real you is bored silly, or seasick, or can't swim, or something. It's because you don't know yourself, you don't know what you really want.'

One evening, he came round with a spare DVD player because Gemma's was playing up. Just as he parked outside the flat, Hazel was coming out of the front door. He wound down the window of his Mercedes SUV.

'She's gone,' said Hazel.

'What d'you mean? Gone where?'

She waved the keys to the flat. 'I'm taking these back to the rental place. Joey came down with a van last night, they packed in all her stuff, she's gone with him . . . I was just checking they hadn't left anything.'

'You're kidding.'

Frank got out of the car, slamming the door, putting all his weight behind it, incandescent with his futile opposition. Passers-by turned to look at him losing his temper and cursing in the street. Hazel reassured him that she thought it was for the best. 'She wasn't exactly making a go of it down here.'

'She needed to give it time. She needed to be patient.'

'Well, maybe.'

Hazel said that she guessed this was goodbye, between them. 'For a while at least. Now that we won't have a reason to meet.'

He offered her a lift to the agency, but she had her own car. Making his farewells, he was so angry at the idea of Gemma's packing up and leaving like that, not even bothering to tell him ('She knew how you'd feel about it,' Hazel explained), that he hardly took in what he was doing or saying. Then, on the road on his way home, the windscreen wipers clearing little wedges of visibility in the suddenly heavy rain, he couldn't remember whether he'd kissed Hazel or not as they parted, or what he'd said to her. Had he only clumsily shaken her hand, after everything they'd been through together? Was it possible he was such a clown? He couldn't forgive himself, and in his chest his heart felt numb and heavy, as if he'd carelessly mislaid something, something good.

Lady Isabella Morpeth's Receipt Book

BY MAEVE HARAN

'So why would our readers be interested in a load of old receipts?' Izzy demanded crossly of her news editor. About to be ex-news editor, as it happened, since he had just told Izzy that, regretfully, after six years as a reporter on their local paper, he was going to have to let her go, which accounted for Izzy's crossness. Not to mention considerable worry, since jobs round here were as hard to find as roses in January. There had been no point protesting that she had a mortgage to pay and a cat to support.

'According to the old bird who contacted us, a receipt is an old-fashioned name for a recipe,' Mark, the news editor, explained. 'It's some ancient book of household hints handed down in her family from generation to generation right back to the year dot.'

'I didn't think women could write in the year dot.'

'Izzy, don't be mean. I would have kept you on till you're eighty if I could. I'll be next, you know.'

Suddenly overcome with worry and emotion, Izzy turned away. She could feel her eczema flaring up, the way it always did when she was stressed, brought on by the thought of being broke and out of work, having to admit to her parents that she had failed again and had another career go wrong for her.

Izzy tried desperately hard not to scratch. She was dark-haired with striking, pale blue eyes and unusually light skin, the kind of skin that stayed red for hours if she scratched it.

'Where does she live then, this old bird?'

'She said Morpeth Hall, but the funny thing is I've worked here fifteen years and I've never heard of it.'

Intrigued despite herself, Izzy sat at her screen and googled 'Morpeth Hall'. Nothing appeared apart from a teacher-training establishment in Lancashire.

'Where did she say it was?'

'Somewhere out on the Alnwick road.'

'OK, I'll have a look.'

'Take the camera. I doubt she'll want to lend us her prize possession.'

'So why did she contact us then?'

'She's had an offer from a museum in London. Quite a lot of money, but she wants it to stay round here. I thought you could launch one of your campaigns. Keep Isabella Morpeth's Receipt Book in the County – that sort of thing.'

Izzy had had a lot of success at rescuing day nurseries from the cuts and stopping wicked developers demolishing ancient greenhouses. Not that she'd managed to save her own job.

Izzy shouldered the office camera and headed for her ancient Fiat. At least it was a nice day. Spring was finally breaking out over the grey stone villages and colouring the dead brownish-purple of the moors. Daffodils were beginning to nod a greeting to wood anemones and even the occasional early foxglove.

It took hours to find Morpeth Hall. She asked three lots of people, who all looked at her as if she were mad. The last one laughed and said, 'You mean old Mrs Morpeth's place?'

He sent her down the valley by a road so narrow she felt she was taking her life in her hands, finally arriving at a small mansion in slate and stone, perfect in its proportions yet still on a human, liveable scale.

Izzy knocked on the door.

Silence.

She knocked again, determined not to have come all this way for nothing, until at last she heard a bolt being pulled back on the inside.

Izzy thought that the person who finally opened the door was a very old man with short iron-grey hair, which he had probably cut himself. It took her a closer look to discover that it was actually a woman, and that the hair had been shaved rather than cut. The woman was tall and extremely thin, wearing a loose tweed suit in shades of purple and dark pink which had clearly been made for her when she was much larger.

She held out her hand, offering a smile of such sweetness that Izzy found herself instantly returning it.

'Are you the girl from the newspaper?' She held out a bony hand. 'Marianne Morpeth. Do come in.'

She stood back to reveal a dramatic hallway where

stag heads competed for space with ancestors in oils against peeling, pale green Chinese wallpaper.

'Excuse the hair, won't you? Brain tumour. Hopefully benign. The Morpeths were always eccentric, so I just thought I was following the family traits. Cup of tea?'

Without waiting for an answer, she led Izzy into the house and down the passage, past a large painting of a striking young woman in a pale pink silk dress laced with ruffles and a huge straw hat tied on with ivory ribbon. But it was her expression that startled Izzy: it was frank, direct and somehow incredibly modern.

'I see you've met Isabella,' commented Marianne, as if Isabella was about to join them for tea. 'It was her receipt book I called the paper about. Started in 1663, just after the Restoration. Every Morpeth added their bit. Unfortunately I'm the last. Milk and sugar?'

She came and stood by Izzy, handing her the tea. 'Don't be fooled by the pink dress – she ruled the household with a rod of iron. There were rules for absolutely everything. Do you want to see her stink room?'

Startled, Izzy followed Marianne Morpeth through the house to a small domed building that resembled a stone igloo. Inside were shelves and a workbench.

'She was a great one for experiments, made all her own medicines and herbal remedies. The country people came from miles around to be treated by Isabella. They happily swallowed anything she gave them – elixir of viper oil, tincture of foxes' lungs, syrup of tobacco. The only thing that really frightened them was in here.'

Marianne threw open the doors to reveal a room with a ceiling painted midnight blue, studded with gold stars over what seemed to be a plunge pool with steps going down to it. 'It's a bath. People didn't have baths then. They thought she was going to drown them. They didn't mind the foxes' lungs. It was the clean water that terrified them.' She laughed to herself. 'Anyway, I expect you'll want to have a proper look at the book.'

Marianne sat Izzy down at a walnut desk next to Isabella's portrait and produced a large volume in faded and splitting red leather. The heady smell of herbs and oils, spiced with cinnamon and larded with goose fat imbibed by the leather over hundreds of years, assaulted her nostrils as she opened it.

As she read through the handwritten pages, Izzy found herself transported back to a world before GP appointments and late-night chemists when the lady of the manor, with her brews of sorrel, rue, feverfew and the roots of dragonwort, or her poultices of bread and whey, were all that stood between the local people and severe illness or an early death.

From time to time she glanced up at Isabella. From the dates listed, it was clear that she had become mistress here at the age of seventeen. Izzy might think herself liberated and independent, yet what of the responsibilities Isabella Morpeth had carried on her silken shoulders at an age when Izzy was still deep in teen magazines?

Soon her notebook was full of instructions on the making of everything from plum cheese, bag pudding and roasted swan to exotic remedies for failing eyesight, mouth ulcers and ague, whatever that was.

Izzy was definitely impressed. She'd never given much thought to ladies of the manor and what they got up to. Lolling around on sofas stitching embroidery or gathering roses while their servants did most of the work, she'd imagined. But Isabella Morpeth's Receipt Book conjured up a very different picture.

Isabella, it was clear, was more of a seventeenth-century businesswoman, managing a large household, preserving food in season, pickling and salting, preparing endless medicines in her stink room. Reading between the lines it was obvious the lord of the manor was often away, and when he was here, was no bloody use to anyone. Isabella had even found time to have seven children, for goodness' sake, though despite all her remedies only one had survived.

Izzy glanced up at the direct gaze of Isabella Morpeth. 'Poor you; how terrible that must have been. By the way, I'm an Isabella too,' she confided silently. 'Not many people know that.'

Izzy finished by taking photographs of the book, and lastly of Isabella herself. She would keep a copy on her mantelpiece.

'You have a look of her, as it happens.' Marianne's voice made her jump. 'Delicate but tough.'

Almost two hours had flashed by before she shook Marianne's hand and headed back to the office, experiencing a strange reluctance to re-enter the modern world.

Mark, the news editor, had no such qualms. 'If you want a full page I'll need your copy by tomorrow.'

'Thanks a lot.'

Izzy was proud of the story when it appeared the following week, especially when the local radio station asked her to come in to talk about it. But contemporary life soon swallowed her up, and she was left with her more pressing worries: the prospect of being jobless and unable to pay her mortgage.

Her eczema flared up spectacularly. 'Ooh, you do look awful,' pointed out Mark, tactlessly.

She only had one more week at work when he put his head round the door. 'Can you write me a quick obituary? Your old lady up at Morpeth Hall, I'm afraid.'

Izzy gazed at him, genuinely shocked. Poor Marianne, the brain tumour must have been malign after all.

'She's left the house and all the paintings to the National Trust.'

Izzy felt a wash of relief that house-clearers wouldn't be sifting through the Hall, bundling up four hundred years of history in crates and black bin liners. And what would have happened to Isabella's portrait? She couldn't bear to think about it.

'Oh, and this came for you.' Mark plonked a Jiffy bag on to Izzy's desk.

She opened it with shaking fingers, hardly able to speak. It was a fat and faded leather tome.

'Wow,' Mark marvelled. 'She's sent you the recipe book.'

A letter fell out, written in a clear if spidery hand, wrapped round a tiny pot containing some sort of cream.

Dear Isabella . . . How had Marianne known Izzy was short for Isabella, a deeply held secret known only to a favoured few? Had she said it out loud when she was communing with the portrait? She was almost sure she hadn't.

I think your namesake would have liked you to have this. I hope you won't mind me including one of her potions. It's made of marigold and hemp oil, mixed with nettle, chickweed and camomile. You'll find the proportions in the book.

Izzy read the label and had to laugh out loud: ' "A Remedy for Ye Scaly Skin". Thanks, Marianne!'

All the same, she rubbed some into the raw rash on her arms and chest.

'The recipe book'll be worth a quid or two,' Mark commented enviously, thumbing through the pages.

But Izzy had no intention of selling. She might see if she could find someone who would be interested in publishing it, though. Failing that, she would put Isabella Morpeth's recipes and remedies on to the

Internet, where others could share them and have the glimpse she'd had into Isabella's vanished world.

She went home with the book clasped to her chest.

'Bloody hell,' Mark, tactful as ever, commented next morning. 'That horrible rash of yours. It's cleared up completely!'

Izzy studied herself. Her skin shone with a pure white radiance, all signs of eczema departed. She threw back her head and laughed.

Maybe Isabella Morpeth, with her stink room and her ancient herbal remedies, had given her something of real value. Suddenly, thanks to Isabella's receipt book, unemployment didn't seem so daunting after all.

A Friend with Benefits

BY VERONICA HENRY

'*O*h, darling, you shouldn't have!'

Rosie smiled up at her husband from her mound of pillows. A breakfast tray, complete with Buck's Fizz, croissants and a perfect red rose, lay on her lap. In her hands was a dark blue apron, emblazoned with the logo of the Mermaid Arms, and tucked into the pocket was a gift voucher.

THE MERMAID ARMS SEAFOOD COOKERY SCHOOL Our weekend courses consist of four 'hands-on' sessions, where you'll be cooking under the supervision of celebrated chef Damien Lee. On Saturday evening, you'll sit down to enjoy the fruits of your labour, along with a glass of two of something cheeky, before trundling up the stairs to our simple but comfortable accommodation overlooking the estuary. On Sunday, you will cook two dishes to take home and enjoy.

'You're always saying you'd love to see him again,' Bill beamed down at her, pride on his face. He'd obviously spent months researching the perfect gift, and she feigned delight so as not to disappoint him. But as she put the voucher back into the pale turquoise envelope, Rosie hoped he wouldn't notice her hands were shaking.

Bill loved telling people, anyone who would listen, 'Of course, Rosie was at university with Damien Lee.' They oohed and aahed and grilled her about his antics, but she revealed nothing other than to say that he was 'good fun'.

Bill would be horrified if he knew the truth. Not that he had thought she was a virgin, exactly, when he met her – she'd been twenty-four – but when Damien first hit the screen a few years ago, she had felt too self-conscious to say, 'Well, of course, we were lovers once.' Then when the scandals began to hit the headlines, she certainly didn't want people to know. She didn't want them wondering what the A-list celebrity chef could possibly have seen in her.

Actually, 'lovers' wasn't entirely accurate. They'd been 'friends with benefits'. That was the modern term. In those days they hadn't given it a name – there hadn't been such an obsession with labelling things back then. They'd shared a chaotic house in Bristol with four other students, and every now and then they went to bed together. No strings attached.

Damien had been a demon in the kitchen even then – when the house threw a supper party, he did the cooking and Rosie did the shopping and chopping. It had been a perfect relationship. When they had graduated, him in Drama and Rosie in French, they had promised to keep in touch, but they hadn't. Of course not.

A demon in the kitchen. And a demon in bed. Rosie's cheeks went pink as she thought about it, all these years later.

Bill put a hand on her knee. 'Happy?' he asked, massaging it lightly. She moved away. She had no intention of expressing her appreciation in that way. The very thought of it made her shudder these days.

Even though she had the perfect husband. Kind, attentive, generous, thoughtful . . . Bill did the washing-up each night, bought her flowers spontaneously; took the recycling out without being reminded. At fifty-two, he was still handsome. So why did she want to run a mile whenever he came close? She picked up the glass of Buck's Fizz and drank, before the hot tears that threatened to sting her eyelids so often these days popped up yet again.

Damien Lee. Rosie had watched his career with horrified fascination. His ambition to be an actor had never panned out, and instead he'd found himself working in the kitchens of some of London's top restaurants. A chance meeting with a documentary producer meant a pilot for a cookery show. *Flash In the Pan* was an overnight hit, and Damien became the thinking woman's brioche.

Of course, his meteoric rise to fame and fortune so late in life meant the press were all over his private life. His marriage collapsed, then he had a string of high-profile relationships with actresses and models. Yet all the time his viewing figures mounted, his book sales escalated, and hc bought the restaurant in Cornwall. Of course people flocked there. Notoriety is a guaranteed pull. The cookery school was booked up for years – it was the must-have gift for the wealthy foodie; the perfect present for a landmark birthday.

Fifty. How had she got to fifty? Rosie sighed, and realised Bill was looking at her anxiously. 'If you don't want to go, you can swap it for something else,' he told her. 'I just thought . . .'

'No, no, it's perfect. I can't wait.' She leaned forward and kissed him on the cheek before slipping out of bed and scuttling into the bathroom as quickly as she could. She knew without looking that Bill would be dejected by her rejection of him, and as usual she felt guilty. Guilty, guilty, guilty.

Three weeks later, she was driving down the M5, her hands clutching the wheel. She hated the motorway – Bill usually did the driving whenever they went away – and she was nervous. She had agonised over her wardrobe before she left, finally settling on a selection of linen trousers and loose tops that accentuated her generous cleavage – the only good thing about her weight gain – accessorised with interesting jewellery to 'distract the eye'.

She was bloody sick of accessorising with interesting jewellery. She longed to wear jeans again, without that unattractive mound of flesh billowing over her waistband. Bill told her that he didn't mind her squodge. Not one bit. Nevertheless, she was horribly conscious that she was three stone heavier than she had been on her graduation day . . . Would Damien recognise her? Or worse, recognise her and not be able to hide the shock on his face?

As she drove over the border into Cornwall, she wondered about not going; checking into an anonymous B&B somewhere. But she couldn't think how to explain to Bill that she had rejected his present, and she couldn't lie – she was a useless liar – so she drove on until she reached the tiny fishing village, then down the steep, winding street until there, in front of her, perched on the harbour, was the Mermaid Arms. The smell of the sea hit her, the sun on the water made her blink and her tummy turned over slowly, once, twice.

She was standing awkwardly in the stainless-steel splendour of the cookery-school kitchen with the rest of the students when Damien arrived. He clocked her immediately.

'Oh my God!' he exclaimed. 'Rosie Sandleford. Where have you been all these years?'

He enveloped her in a huge hug. He'd always been demonstrative. A hugger. A kisser. It was the drama student in him.

'Rosie Prior now,' she managed to squeak.

Damien smiled round at the others. 'This girl was my absolute best friend at university.' He turned back to her, holding her hands, inspecting her. 'We have so much to catch up on.'

'I think I know most of what's happened to you,' she told him, smiling under his attention, and he threw his eyes up to heaven.

'The bloody press,' he said. 'I'm not the monster they make me out to be.'

Rosie gestured to the rest of the room, conscious that they were all gawping at them. 'This lot aren't here to listen to us reminisce . . .'

Damien didn't need telling twice. For the rest of the day he held his students spellbound as he unveiled his secrets. He sliced and diced with precision, his deadly knives boning and filleting and skinning at lightning speed. Rosie marvelled at how deftly he handled the tools of his trade; the careless confidence with which he threw a whole skate into a puddle of melting butter at just the right moment. Under his instruction, they made caper mayonnaise and salsa verde; boiled up bones and shells to make stock for bouillabaisse. And at seven o'clock they all sat down at the long refectory table and shared spaghetti *vongole*, and scallops in garlic butter, and brill braised in Prosecco.

Afterwards, Damien insisted that Rosie come up to his private apartment for a nightcap. They sat on his balcony as a golden sun shimmied towards the sea. He brought out a bottle of *vin santo* and a plate of pistachio biscotti and they sat chatting companionably. She'd forgotten how he used to make her laugh. How easy it was to be herself with him. He made her feel comfortable in her own skin. She hadn't felt like that for a long time.

As she dunked her fourth biscotti into the luscious liquid, Damien leaned forward and looked straight at her.

'Are you happy, Rosie?'

She paused, the biscotti halfway to her mouth. What was she supposed to say? She sighed.

'I have a husband who loves me. I have a beautiful house. Four wonderful children. Everything I want . . .'

'But . . . ?'

She shrugged. She didn't know what to say, because she herself hadn't been able to put a finger on it. She didn't know where it had come from: her lack of confidence, the overwhelming sense that she had lost herself somewhere. . .

To her horror, a tear rolled out of her eye and plopped on to her hand.

'Hey.' Alarmed, Damien got to his feet, and before she knew it he had wrapped her up in his arms. 'I didn't mean to make you cry.'

'Sorry,' she murmured, her face pressed up against the comfort of his white linen shirt. 'It's all I seem to do these days.'

He ran his fingers along the soft creamy flesh of her bare arm. If Bill had done that, she would have moved away. Subtly, so as not to hurt his feelings. But this felt different. She swallowed. Was this a gesture of comfort? As he held her and stroked her, she felt herself melting. Warmth slid down her like honey dripping from a spoon. The moon came out from behind a cloud and illuminated them.

Damien's lips were on her neck. She thought she might die from the pleasure of it.

'Rosie, Rosie, Rosie,' he whispered.

'Don't,' she whispered, praying he wouldn't stop.

'It's not as if it's infidelity,' he replied. 'We're already lovers. It really wouldn't count.'

What on earth did he want with her? A middle-aged housewife riddled with wrinkles and stretch marks and grey hairs and thread veins, some of which she'd managed to cover up?

'Why?' she asked him as his hand slid under her top and massaged the flesh at the top of her waistband. She cringed and pushed him away. 'Why would you want me? You could have anyone you wanted . . ."

He looked at her in surprise.

'Look at me!' she cried. 'I'm an overweight, frumpy, boring lump.'

As she said it, she heard how ridiculous she sounded. Self-pity was never attractive, she knew that.

'Sorry,' she said, managing a shaky laugh. 'I shouldn't have pointed that out, should I? You might not have noticed.'

As she wiped away the tears that had betrayed her, Damien looked at her in disbelief.

'You really have no idea how gorgeous you are, do you?' he asked. 'You're open, you're fun, you're natural – you embrace everything life has to offer. You love people. You've made friends with everyone today. They'll go home remembering you – your warmth, your kindness . . .' He pulled her back into his arms. 'You're beautiful, Rosie,' he murmured, running his fingers through her curls. 'You always were, and you still are. I hope your husband knows how lucky he is.'

She tipped back her head, revelling in the feeling of coming back to life. She'd thought she'd closed down for ever; as if some greater power had flipped the switch to 'off'. Every time Bill came close she felt guilty for pushing him away, but she couldn't bear the thought of close contact; anyone trying to get pleasure from her worn-out, battle-weary body.

Yet here was a man who could have any woman in the world, telling her she was gorgeous. And she didn't think it was just a line. The press might paint him as a womanising monster, but she knew Damien only too well. He was never disingenuous. Silver-tongued, yes, but she knew he meant every word.

He was holding her by the hand, leading her to the bedroom.

'I haven't done it for . . . for over a year,' she whispered. 'I can't face it. I can't bear myself. This is the first time I've felt even remotely like it for months. And it's wrong, Damien. It's wrong. I can't . . .'

'No one would know.'

He was gazing into her eyes. Her tummy flipped again. 'No,' she said softly. 'But I would.'

*

When she got home, the house was immaculate, the lawns were mowed and Bill was waiting with a large gin and tonic and a smile on his face.

'I want to hear all about it.'

'Hang on,' she replied. 'I need to get all this in the freezer.'

She took the dishes she had made that day out of the cool box and went into the kitchen.

She slid the monkfish wrapped in pancetta inside, marking the date carefully with a thick black pen. It would do perfectly for their anniversary supper in three weeks' time.

Before she went back into the garden, she checked herself in the cloakroom mirror. Her eyes were sparkling like the sea in front of the Mermaid Arms. It was all she had needed: a boost to her ego, a vote of confidence from someone whose opinion she valued. Not HRT, or plastic surgery, or a shrink.

A friend with benefits indeed.

Then she went back out into the garden, slid her arms around her husband's neck and kissed him like she meant it.

Christmas Getaway

BY VICTORIA HISLOP

*A*n airport in December. It was probably the most intensely 'seasonal' environment on earth, with its relentlessly cheerful music and glittering decorations. Lizzie steeled herself. For the first time ever, she would be alone at Christmas. 'Are you hanging up a stocking on your wall?' blared out from an invisible sound system, and a sales assistant in flashing reindeer antlers thrust out a sample of 'Mistletoe'. *Perfect for (Se)Xmas!* said the poster behind her.

When they said 'two hours prior to departure', Lizzie always added an extra one. She liked to be relaxed and to do last-minute shopping. For a while, she stood and scrutinised the departures board, reading the names of all the destinations, both exotic and mundane, and mentally, she gave each one a tick or a cross, according to whether she wanted to go.

Her own destination was on the board: Phuket. It seemed a good place to go at Christmas: guaranteed sunshine, fresh fish and not even the possibility of hearing Noddy Holder. She was going on a yoga and meditation retreat, so she knew there would be plenty of singles like herself needing a focus for their day and intent on self-improvement. She was fairly certain that an ashram would not appeal to honeymoon couples.

She took the escalator to her favourite coffee shop, taking a seat where the departures board remained in sight, and opened the book she had just bought: *Introduction to Yoga and Meditation*. She had gone to the gym a lot more this year, not because she needed to lose weight – that had happened very speedily after the break-up – but only as a way of killing time. Even so, she doubted she would ever achieve the lotus position.

Every five minutes or so she looked up at the board. As soon as the gate opened, she would make her way over, anxious to be the first on the plane.

In the warm, windowless world of the departure lounge, she looked up and saw that the flight before hers was delayed and felt a moment of pity for the people who would arrive late at their destination.

She could hardly wait to leave and looked forward so much to the limbo of hanging in the air, for a while being nowhere before she was somewhere once again. It was the most relaxing place in the world, a location without a locale, somewhere but nowhere. Perhaps this was what she was looking for. Maybe yoga would be the same; a mental journey to temporary oblivion. A time to forget and perhaps to move on as well.

The next time she looked up, there were so many people gathered under the screen that she could not see it. She stood on her seat to look over their heads and saw the reason for the ripples of consternation that swept around the airport. In the few minutes between noticing the delay of that first flight and getting up to buy a second coffee, the board had changed. From one second to the next, electronically, inaudibly, every flight, even those that had been 'Boarding' had changed to 'Delayed'.

Paris, Tenerife, New York, Kingston, and then . . . Phuket.

Wherever they were going, short or long haul, no one would be taking off on time.

People began to talk to each other, stranger to stranger, foreigners attempting questions in broken English, everyone bonded by the common catastrophe. There was one person who had only just come through passport control who was not surprised by the situation.

Harry never liked to give himself any more than half an hour in an airport, but today he wished he had not left himself so short of time. A few flakes of snow had begun to fall. At first they were almost unnoticeable, but soon they had increased and within moments he had found himself enveloped in a blizzard, with snow flying horizontally towards him, swirling around his car as, along with the thousands of others heading for their Christmas getaway, he found himself slowing to less than ten miles per hour. It was as if they were inside a child's snow-scene toy and someone had picked it up and shaken it. By the time he steered himself into the multistorey car park, there were four inches of snow on his roof. He carefully stood back as he slammed the car door, avoiding the fall of snow on his flip-flops. He always dressed for his destination, and that day had raised the temperature in his car to match Jamaican heat.

Thank God I'm going to the sun, he thought to himself, reaching into his boot and removing a small suitcase. He got into the terminal without even a flake of snow on him, and went straight to the First Class lounge where he was swiftly served with a glass of champagne. Sinking down into a comfortable seat in the overheated lounge, he began to peruse his newspaper, but soon he had drifted away, relaxed by the effects of alcohol and the warmth of the room.

In the café, Lizzie was trying to hold back her tears. The situation outside had worsened. One by one, the planes were being cancelled. Willing hers to be the exception, she stared at the board before the inevitable happened.

Clearly there had been a blanket instruction, a response to the blanket of snow that had now dumped itself on the entire south of England. There was nothing any of these angry passengers could do, but this did not stop them complaining and shouting and trying to find someone to blame. Seasonal good cheer had vanished.

But it wasn't even snowing three hours ago, Lizzie thought to herself. She hadn't even had to scrape ice off her windscreen. It had been a bit chilly, but nowhere near to freezing.

A loudspeaker announcement told passengers that it was likely the motorway would reopen in the next hour once the snowploughs had been through, but there would be no landings or take-offs until further notice.

Lizzie sat there. Quietly. Of all the destinations in all the world, the last place she wanted to go was home – a place with an empty fridge and bad memories. She watched as people in various states of fury and frustration began to make their way back out through passport control, to reverse all the processes they had gone through earlier that morning: to uncheck themselves in, to reclaim luggage, to convert their money back again into sterling. It did not take long for people to begin pushing and shoving, eager to be at the front of one of the many queues they would need to join.

Swiftly, the airport descended into chaos.

'Mr Montague . . . Mr Montague . . .'

Someone was gently shaking Harry's arm.

'Mr Montague . . . I'm so sorry to have to wake you.'

'What?' He sat up, momentarily disorientated. 'What's happening?'

'I'm afraid they have cancelled . . . all flights . . . the blizzard . . . I'm so sorry.'

'Oh.'

'And we're shutting the lounge now, as everyone needs to try and make their way home. The motorways have been cleared, but there could well be another fall, and we don't want to get stuck here, do we?'

The woman's tone was artificially jolly, but Harry failed to smile as her words sank in. Home. For Christmas. Nothing could have filled him with greater misery.

What would he do? What would he eat? Who would he see? There was nothing for him at home.

'We have an arrangement for all First Class passengers with the Meridian Hotel,' she said. 'So there will be a room there if you need one.'

Eventually he could see that the hostess was serious. She was closing up. The rows of neat canapés had disappeared and the bottles were locked away. He picked up his newspaper, purchased less than an hour before, and got up to leave.

It was eerily quiet outside in the corridor, and as he came into the brightly lit expanse he saw that all the shops were shuttered, empty café chairs were neatly positioned around tables and the tills were silent.

The terminal was empty. Except for one person. A woman sitting alone on a banquette, very still, apparently waiting for someone. She heard him approach across the silence, the slight squeak of his rubber-soled flip-flops alerting her. She turned round.

'Harry . . . ?'

'Lizzie! God! Lizzie . . .'

Their dismay and surprise was mutual. Of all the people in all the world that they had least wanted or expected to see, it was each other.

He sat down opposite her, keeping his distance, noting the change in her appearance since he had last seen her. Her hair was much shorter and blonder, and she seemed smaller, certainly slimmer. But her eyes were the same dazzling blue.

Only the previous Christmas they had been together at Harry's family home, enjoying dinner with his parents and anticipating a big New Year party at their own place.

They had been engaged. The date had been set and guests sent the 'Keep the Date' cards. But something had gone wrong. By mistake she had picked up his phone on Christmas Day (their BlackBerrys were identical) and found a message from someone called Sue, who apparently worked in his office. It was flirtatious, intimate, with terms of endearment for him and nicknames that she did not recognise.

The first time it happened, she said nothing. But when she found another, two days later, she confronted him. The row escalated. She would not accept his denials and stormed out, refusing to accept his explanation that they had been sent to the wrong number. She simply did not believe him. For months he rang her every day, but she rejected every call.

Now, for the first time in a year, they were standing face to face in an empty terminal, obliged to speak.

'Look, Lizzie. Do you notice something?' he asked.

She stared at him in silence.

'I'm on my own.'

She noticed that, as ever, even for long-haul flights, he travelled light. She knew his passport and wallet would be inside one of the buttoned pockets on the side of his shorts, and that he would watch films throughout the flight. He could never read on planes. But he still had a copy of the *Guardian* with which he would have killed time for ten minutes in the lounge, and she took in that it was still folded to the page he had been reading.

'And look—'

He held the page in front of her. She turned her head away. She had no wish to see him or to listen to anything he had to say.

'Look, Lizzie. Look! Please!'

She took the paper from him, and without looking at Harry scanned the page he had been reading.

Lonely Hearts, it said at the top. And underneath she could see that he had ringed one of the small ads.

'I'm still looking, you see. Still trying to find some-one else to replace you. And this is what I've had to do . . .'

She read the one entry that he had ringed.

Blonde, blue-eyed. 35. Loves Bob Dylan and the blues. And classical music too. Heart still mending but ready for new love.

'You see who I am still looking for? Lizzie? Some-one just like you! Don't you see?'

With a slight reluctance, she looked again and her eyes focused on the four-line entry.

'Yes,' she said, abashed. 'I do see. It's someone just like me.'

Most people were on the road by now, speeding along the freshly cleared motorway before the next predicted fall. Harry left his car where it was, and he and Lizzie walked along the passageway that connected the airport to an adjacent hotel. Apart from a few stranded foreigners, they were the last ones to check in. There was nowhere in the world they would rather be.

As the Time Draws Near

BY EOWYN IVEY

*T*here are more ways to die in this place than a woman can count.

Ridgemont Glacier calves, and crushes two sightseeing kayakers. A drunken man wanders from his village in the night and freezes to death alone on the tundra. A Bush pilot lands to deliver supplies at a remote cabin and the paranoid cabin-dweller shoots him with a 30-06 hunting rifle as the pilot steps out of the plane. A young mother wraps her newborn baby against her chest beneath her parka and heads out on a snow-mobile to visit a neighbour, but when she arrives she discovers that the infant has been smothered to death, a tiny trail of blood dribbling from its nose. On Kodiak Island a teenage boy shoots his first deer, but the bullet passes through the animal and hits and kills his father, who is standing in the brush on the other side. Two girls drown while trying to canoe the Matanuska River.

Piper's father falls out of the sky.

Her entire life she had been waiting for this news, though she didn't know what form it would take. She had long since fled Alaska, but continued to watch from afar – television broadcasts, the Anchorage news-paper, emails from old friends. She marvelled at the spinning, diving, spectacular deaths. She watched and waited and wondered: how long could a daredevil like her father survive when there were so many ways to die?

'Take a look at that.' The Bush pilot's voice fills her earphones, distant and muffled as if coming from another world. The left wing dips and the small, shut-tering plane leans to the side. The pilot nods down-ward.

Far below on the Alaska tundra several bull caribou run along a thin, twisting game trail. The pilot drops the plane to get a closer look. Piper's stomach ripples with nausea. The caribou turn from the trail and begin to run faster, their antlers bone white like branches of driftwood raised to the sky.

'Beautiful,' she says into her headset. Because that's what her father would have said, and he would have peered over his Ray-Ban sunglasses and shook his head in disbelief, as if he hadn't seen a thousand caribou like these. And then he would have been off, pulling the plane back up and out over the tundra, grinning like this was all some grand adventure that would never end.

The metal box holding his ashes is a cold weight in Piper's lap.

. . . stalled on take-off . . . sorry to inform you . . . the plane stalled on take-off . . .

The early-morning sun pools in the tundra ponds

beneath the wings of the airplane, and as far as she can see in any direction the earth is made of rust-coloured flatlands broken up by odd-shaped, glistening slices of water. Then the pilot changes altitude slightly, the ground shifts beneath her and instead of silver sunlight, the ponds below reflect dark blue sky and strips of white clouds. The small airplane's engine roars violently in her head and a patch of turbulence causes her seat to jump and lurch. She closes her eyes and holds on to the metal box.

'Is Tuttle expecting you out there?' the pilot asked when she called to book the flight.

'No. I'm sure he isn't,' she said.

'Because he's not your warm, fuzzy type. If you show up there unexpected, the old man is likely to run you off.'

But she has no choice. Tucked in with the maps and pilot directory in the pocket behind the seat of her father's destroyed Super Cub airplane had been a will, signed and dated June 21, 1991 – the year Piper graduated from high school and left Alaska. Twenty years, he had carried it with him. He had even gone as far as to have it laminated in plastic so that it might survive a water crash. It was simple and to the point: *I, Red Robertson, leave everything I have to my daughter, Piper Robertson. I want her to cremate me and take my ashes out to Ernest Tuttle's place and spread them beneath the spruce tree. He'll know which one. Unless he's dead, too. Then just dump me at his doorstep and say a prayer for both of us.*

Though he didn't include it in the will, Piper suspected her father would have wanted a drunken wake on his behalf, too. She remembered when she was a little girl and Red's best friend Braden died in an avalanche. It was December. Dark and cold. The grown-ups gathered in a circle on frozen Wolverine Lake and recited poetry – Robert Service and Walt Whitman. *Perhaps soon, some day or night while I am singing, my voice will suddenly cease.* Then they built a bonfire on the snowy shore and got drunk on beer and whiskey while the children ran wild like heathens and waved flaming spruce boughs in the darkness. Late that night, or maybe early the next morning, Red fired up his snowmobile. Someone brought out Alpine skis and a long tether, and they took turns pulling each other around on the lake, the snowmobile on full throttle, flying across the pitch-black ice. There was a mad, grinning danger to it that frightened Piper. The grown-ups stood on the ice and laughed and shook their heads. Even at six years old, though, she was perplexed. Why throw yourselves headlong into cold death when it is already hunting you down?

It was a question that never left her.

'This is Lieutenant Dan Richards with the Alaska State Troopers. I'm calling about your father, Red Robertson. I'm sorry to inform you that he was killed yesterday afternoon . . . I'm sorry, ma'am . . . The investigation is ongoing, but it appears that the airplane was overloaded and the plane stalled on take-off.'

Of course. That is how her father would die. Diving. Reeling. Overloaded.

The landing is terrifying, and the pilot warns her before he begins the descent.

'This is a tight airstrip. Hold on to your hat.'

The term 'airstrip' is an embellishment. A month ago, the pilot said, the stretch of dry riverbed was beneath three feet of rushing water. When the river level dropped, the sand bar emerged and now allows for a short, rough landing in a narrow, rocky valley. The plane bounces on its balloon-like tyres and comes to a sudden stop not far from the edge of the spruce forest.

'Yeehaw! Here we are. That landing always wakes me up.'

She climbs out of the plane. Her legs are wobbly and she has the sudden desire to lie down.

'Go on up – see if Tuttle is around before I take off. I've got some goat hunters waiting for me to pull them out of Knik Valley, then I'll be back for you.'

The cabin is visible through the trees, set back from the river. Piper walks unsteadily across the sand, carrying the metal box under one arm, and finds a trail through the willows. She follows it up the steep embankment and into the spruce forest.

The cabin is small and dark and made of peeled logs and a sod roof; it looks like it sprouted from the woods.

There is no sign of Ernest Tuttle, but the leather-hinged door is ajar.

'Hello? Mr Tuttle? Hello?'

'Who the hell are you?'

The old man steps out of the cabin with a rifle in his hands. He raises it to his waist and aims it at her.

'I said, who the hell are you?'

'I'm . . . I'm Piper Robertson. I think you knew my father, Red?'

He squints his eyes, shakes his head slowly. And then he sighs, leans his rifle against the door frame and rubs his forehead with the palm of one hand.

'I don't suppose you come with good news.'

'No, Mr Tuttle. I'm afraid not.'

He was racing bad weather and overloaded his Super Cub with the last load of meat and supplies from a moose-hunting camp. He had no passengers. When he took off from the mountain ridge, the plane stalled and fell into a nosedive. There wasn't enough time to recover.

'Dad said something in his will about wanting to have his ashes spread by a certain spruce tree. He said you would know where.'

'Yep. I do,' Tuttle says. 'I'll show you.'

The woods are quiet, and she inhales the scent of her childhood – sun-warmed spruce needles, mountain air, moss. Small red berries dot the forest floor. White flowers bloom on a large plant. She used to know all their names, but has forgotten them. She follows the old man along the river's edge, and then up from the valley and towards the steep, rocky cliffs.

When they reach the top of a rise, a cold breeze blows off the river, glacial and pure. She hasn't breathed air like this in a very long time. It brings tears to her eyes. The old man stops in front of a large spruce tree, but he doesn't speak.

'Is this it?' she asks. 'It's nice. But why here, I mean, of all the places Dad has been?'

'We knew each other a long time. He saved my hide more than once, flying in and out of here when I needed him. He liked this part of the river. He used to say if he had been a settling-down kind of guy, he would have called it home. I remember when your mother died – he brought some of her ashes out here. He put them at the base of this spruce tree. It was a little sapling then, and he liked to think it was the same age as you.'

'I had no idea.'

''Course not. You were just a baby.'

'Three. I was three years old. And he always told me Mom's ashes were back in Colorado with her family.'

'Yep. Her folks wanted to put her to rest down there. But he snuck some ashes, just a thimbleful, really, and sprinkled them right here. I think this is where he would have liked to see you grow up, with him and your mother. If things had been different. He said he always pictured a little cabin facing out to the river, you on a tyre swing, your mother in the garden.

He had a big heart, you know. Loved you two like there was no tomorrow.'

Piper shrugs, though she knows it's true. All she can feel is a kind of hot, sobbing anger that reminds her of her adolescence.

'I never understood. If he cared so much about me, why did he take all those chances? He was all I had.'

Tuttle puts his hands in his pockets and turns to face the river.

'It's the damnedest thing,' he says. 'I've got a black bear shadowing me. Last few weeks or so. He pops up along the river every few days. Yesterday he and I ran sideways of each other along this trail. I couldn't get a good look at him, but he was in those alders there, following me, like maybe he was wondering how good I'd be to eat.'

Piper fidgets with the metal box. Why did she think the old man would be any help at all?

'I'll bet your dad always told you if you've got a black bear after you, you don't go running and shrieking. That just whets his appetite. Your fear makes him want you all the more. He'll chase you down. Try to hamstring you. Swipe at your back and knock you to the ground. Then you're done for. No,' he says slowly, 'you can't outrun him.'

For the first time, she looks into his eyes – old and watery with faded blue irises. But there is a gentle sadness she hadn't noticed before.

'Your dad knew there was no running. So he wanted to face it down. Look right into those black eyes and let it know he wasn't afraid. Even if he was. He wanted the beast to believe that he would go down fighting, eye to eye, and that he was so crazy he was even looking forward to the fight. Maybe then your dad could chase it off, even if it was just for a little while longer.'

Piper crouches beneath the spruce branches and opens the metal box. The fine, grey powder inside reminds her of the ashes from the woodstove when she was a child. She tips the box until the ashes begin to spill on to the ground, over exposed roots and layers of spruce needles. She tries to recall a line from a poem or a verse from the Bible. But all she can envision is her dad locked in a standing embrace with a black bear, like two Greco-Roman wrestlers. The bear is all roar and claw and teeth and glistening black fur, and there is her dad. Punching. Hollering. Fighting with everything he has.

She latches the metal box and follows Tuttle down the trail. Neither of them speaks, and Piper is glad for the silence, the forest and the river.

When they near the cabin, Tuttle stops in the trail.

'Look at that,' he says quietly. 'There's that fellow just now.'

Piper searches the sky, expecting to see the airplane, but Tuttle is looking toward the river.

On the other side, a black bear paces at the shore. It stops, turns, walks along the water's edge and turns again, as if it were thinking of swimming across. Then it stands on its hind legs and puts its muzzle into the air.

Piper imagines her father charging across the river at the bear. The water splashes around him, shining and glistening. He grins and yells and when he hits the far shore, he starts throwing punches.

But she is nothing like her father. Even from here, the black bear a dark figure in the distance, all she wants to do is run.

Internet Dating

BY CATHY KELLY

*I*t was the fault of the kitchen radiator. Long, modern, set vertically on the wall, and radiating a smidge of heat down low while being icicle-cold up high.

Kerry could handle most household maintenance these days. After the divorce, she'd bought her own toolkit and now, three years later, could do almost anything – except drain the radiators.

'Men understand these sorts of things,' said her mother, Julia, shivering in a navy shift dress and a thin cashmere wrap in Kerry's bright kitchen. 'If I didn't have Marcus, I don't know what I would do.'

Marcus had replaced Tony, who'd replaced Sean, who'd replaced . . .

Kerry often lost track of her mother's complicated love life. In the thirty years since Kerry's father had died, Julia had been very happy with a stream of admiring men who took her to dinner and on gorgeous holidays cruising the world. 'Easy to have a succession of admiring men,' Kerry thought crossly, poking around in the kitchen's dump-it drawer for something resembling a radiator key, 'if you were as beautiful at seventy-four as you had been at thirty.'

Her mother had the bone structure of a ballerina and clearly had been at the Botox, although it was very subtly done. Tall and elegant in her cashmere with her silvery-grey hair, she resembled the type of model Marks & Spencers used in their Christmas campaigns.

'You need a man about the house, Kerry,' her mother said finally, looking round the kitchen decorated with her daughter's bright oils of every flower imaginable. 'I've been saying it for three years, and I'm going to say it again. You can't spend the rest of your life rattling between the office and painting in the garden shed. And your clothes . . .'

Julia's gaze travelled up Kerry's painting outfit: old, loose jeans and a sweatshirt, both ingrained with oil paint and turpentine.

Kerry had changed after work, and planned to fit in a couple of hours in her shed-cum-studio working on a canvas from some photos of crimson arum lilies. She was due to have her first show in a month.

'The Internet's the place to find men,' announced Millie, Kerry's daughter, who'd breezed into the room without them noticing. She dumped her college rucksack on the kitchen table.

'Gran, you look fab, as usual.'

'Jean Muir dress. I still fit into it,' said her grandmother happily, doing a twirl. 'And you're looking pretty lovely yourself, Millie.' Julia hugged her granddaughter, who'd inherited both her bone structure and her height.

When the three of them went out together, Kerry – short, round-faced and fighting a constant battle to hold on to some sort of waist in the face of menopausal hormones – often felt like a changeling dropped into M&S Advert World.

'Yes, I've heard great things about these dating sites,' agreed Julia. 'Or you could join a supper club. My school friend Nora did that. Better than putting a picture up on the Internet. Nora needs people to meet her and discover her lovely personality rather than put a photo up, which puts them off,' she added, neatly diminishing Nora.

'You have to watch how the men describe themselves,' Millie said. 'If they mention the word "cuddly" or say they like romantic nights in, it means they need a year of Weight Watchers and can't afford to take you out.'

Kerry burst out laughing.

'I could do with Weight Watchers myself,' she said.

'Don't say that,' Millie said, shocked. 'They'll run like the clappers. No, you say you're a mature, artistic lady . . .'

Kerry laughed even louder at this.

'I sound like a madam in a brothel, floating round in chiffon.'

Millie and Julia exchanged looks.

'I'll talk to my friend Belinda,' said Julia finally. 'Her son's recently back in Ireland. Nasty divorce, I hear.

He'll be snapped up in a shot, so you could get a crack at him before everyone else does.'

Kerry closed her eyes briefly, thinking of how peaceful it would be in the shed with her beloved Nina Simone playing and no talk of snapping up recently divorced men.

Millie worked on her mother's dating profile for the Internet site, while Kerry looked for plumbers.

'Does "no job too small" mean they won't charge a horrendous call-out fee for draining my radiators?' she asked Millie.

Millie wasn't listening. 'I'm going to say late forties. Early fifties can translate into late fifties, and all these men seem to want twenty-four-year-olds to have fun with.'

'Welcome to my world,' muttered Kerry.

But Millie wasn't even listening.

'And I can't say you're five foot two, can I, Mum? Written down like that, it makes you sound like a munchkin.'

'No, go ahead,' insisted her mother, making a list of plumbers. 'Say munchkin. Munchkin who has had enough of men and has to eat her body weight in chocolate every day or she goes mad.'

'Mum,' implored Millie. 'You're not taking this seriously. Gran's right. Dad's happily settled, and there's no reason why you can't be.'

'Apart from being a munchkin who wears bad clothes and can't drain her own radiators,' Kerry finished for her. 'Darling, I'm not sure I'm ready for dating yet. Or ever, if it comes to that. I'm happy as I am.'

'Denial is not a river in Egypt,' said Millie, and went back to composing the perfect advert.

Julia and Millie chose Kerry's first man for her.

'He looks charming,' said Julia, peering at the photo.

'Plus he owns his own business,' said Millie, who was studying business and had decided that a self-made man was just what her mother needed.

'Probably has a business growing marijuana under heat lamps,' muttered Kerry, but the other two didn't hear her.

Despite her protests, a date was set up, Julia went with her on a painful dress-purchasing excursion and on the great evening in question, Millie used the hot rollers on her mother's hair to make her look date-ready.

'Phone if you need us,' Julia told her daughter as she and Millie pushed Kerry out her own front door.

'Don't go into the car park with him,' Millie warned.

'And if he has a room booked, tell him he should be ashamed of himself!' Julia added.

She and Millie were going to sit in and watch a film on TV, and Kerry wished she were watching it with them. She didn't want to be haring off to a local hotel to sit in the lobby and look meaningfully at all men wearing dark suits with red ties, which was what Ned was supposed to be wearing.

There seemed to be a red-tie-wearing convention in town that night, and Kerry felt as if she'd eyeballed every single one of the convention delegates before her date turned up.

'I thought it was you,' said a short, bald man, sliding into the seat beside her and pressing a sweaty hand into hers. 'I'm Ned. I'm sorry I'm late. Business, you know.'

For an instant, Kerry thought of saying, 'I'm not Kerry, I'm waiting for my husband/lover/psychiatrist,' anything to escape this man who was nothing like the 'charming, debonair high-flyer' in the advert, or the man in the photo. But she didn't.

Instead, she said, 'Hello, lovely to meet you,' even though it wasn't.

Over two white-wine spritzers, Ned told her about his divorce, how his ex-wife was taking him to the cleaners, how he hadn't used his own photo in the advert – 'nobody does, you know' – and that he had this timeshare apartment in Portugal and his two-week slot was in about a month.

'Really?' said Kerry, wondering why was she doing this in the first place. To please her mother and Millie, that was why. Well, if they wanted to date Ned, they were welcome to him.

She got to her feet and smiled.

'Ned, you're going to make some woman very happy, but I think we're not suited. I'm not a two-weeks-in-Portugal kind of woman. I'm more of a week-in-Connemara sort of person. Might as well not start off on false pretences. I'm sure it'll be easy as pie to find a gorgeous woman to head off on holidays with you. Here's money for my share of the drinks.'

Beaming as she slapped fifteen euros on the table, she grabbed her bag and walked at high speed out of the hotel.

After Kerry had explained to her mother and daughter just how utterly untruthful Ned had been in his Internet advert, they got the message.

'Things happen for a reason,' Kerry said. 'I don't want a date, so the universe didn't give me one.'

'You and your universe,' sighed Julia as she left that night. 'Things don't simply happen, Kerry, darling – you have to make them happen.'

Kerry hugged her mother. 'I don't want this to happen, Mum,' she said. 'I'm happy the way I am. Honestly.'

That night, she checked the local web guide for plumbers and sent messages to a couple of them, explaining that she wanted a few radiators drained.

Next morning, only one had replied. There was no call-out fee, he said: he'd charge simply for the time it took him, and was she free the following evening at six?

The plumber was called Sam, a handsome man of about her age, with a shock of salt-and-pepper hair and a relaxed, easy smile.

A cup of tea would be gratefully received, he said, when she'd shown him the first chilly radiator.

'Beautiful paintings,' he said, looking round at the walls with interest. 'Are they yours?'

Kerry beamed.

'Yes,' she said. 'A gallery owner has invited me and a couple of other artist friends to have an exhibition at his place next month. I need fifteen paintings, one more to go – but I'm sort of stuck on these arum lilies.'

'It's hard to paint to order, though, isn't it?' said Sam, settling down at the kitchen radiator and laying out his tools.

'Yes,' she agreed. 'How do you know that?'

He shrugged, his back still to her.

'I used to paint a bit. Still do, but it's tough making a living out of it any more. Hence the plumbing.'

'I'm sorry,' began Kerry.

'Don't be.' Sam turned and smiled at her. 'Painting can make you spend too much time on your own, and when you've just moved in with your mother she thinks she can talk endlessly about why you got divorced, and if she could only set you up with someone else . . . Sorry. You don't want to hear my problems.'

'Sounds a bit like my problems,' Kerry said cheerfully.

'You too?' he said.

'Three years ago.'

She watched him expertly drain her radiators, and

thought of asking him to teach her how to do it. But if she did that, he wouldn't need to come back, would he?

Doing the dining-room radiator, they talked easily about children, divorce and family members who wanted them paired off like animals in the ark.

'My mother and my daughter made me go on an Internet date,' Kerry said, 'and I'm not ready for that yet.'

'But you wouldn't mind dating someone?' Sam asked, looking at her.

He had a lovely smile. And he seemed to be smiling at her a lot in an admiring way, she decided happily. As if he fancied her.

She took a deep breath.

'I prefer to think the right person will come my way when I'm ready,' Kerry said softly. 'Does that sound silly?'

'That's not silly at all,' said Sam quietly. 'That's what I think. I'm trying to explain that to my mother, who's driving me demented trying to set me up with her friend's daughter. Apparently, this daughter spends too much time alone—' He stopped abruptly. 'Paint-ing.'

They stared at each other.

'I don't suppose your mother's name is Belinda, is it?' asked Kerry.

Sam grinned.

'And your mother's Julia?'

This time, Kerry grinned.

'The universe does work in mysterious ways, doesn't

it?' She took the plunge. 'I don't suppose you have time to stay for a coffee after you've drained my radiators?'

'I couldn't think of anything I'd like more,' Sam said sincerely.

We'll Always Have Paris

BY CATHY KELLY

*P*aris, declared Hettie, slamming down the magazine she was reading in Emily's kitchen. A weekend in Paris was the answer. 'The answer to what?' asked Emily, absently stirring the soup she was heating up for their lunch.

'The answer to our holidays, and what I'm going to do with Sheila when she comes to stay,' said Hettie in astonishment, as if Emily must have been asleep for the past ten minutes while Hettie had been hatching her plan.

Being used to your sister's flights of fancy and being in the mood for them were two entirely different things. For a full fifty-six years, Emily had experienced Hettie's quicksilver brain and her habit of loudly reaching conclusions without ever actually explaining what she was planning in the first place.

Normally, Emily listened patiently but in the year since James had died, she found she had no patience left for anyone. Not even her beloved sister.

'Let me get this straight,' she said. 'You're suggesting that you, me and your old school friend, whom you haven't seen for donkey's years, should go to Paris on my thirtieth anniversary weekend?' Emily said.

She felt the familiar pain in her chest, the heavy weight that seemed to crush her heart and her soul at the thought of her thirtieth wedding anniversary. 'Are. You. Insane, Hettie?'

The old Emily would never have spoken like that. But the old Emily had been lost the day James had suffered a massive heart attack while driving to work. She'd never had the chance to say goodbye, never been able to hold his hand and tell him that she was with him. He'd died in the ambulance, and all that was left for Emily was to sit beside his dead body in the hospital and stroke the leonine mane of silver hair he was so proud of having, even though his two brothers were entirely bald.

'See,' he used to say, grinning at her as he brushed his hair, 'not bad for an old guy.'

James had never lived to be an old guy. He was sixty-one, four years away from retirement and full of the plans they had.

Round-the-world cruises: 'If we win the lottery,' Emily laughed.

'Lots of bus tours if we don't,' James would counter. 'We'll figure it out. Teamwork, darling.'

Grief was a strange beast. It hijacked her at the oddest moments – just when she'd thought that perhaps, just perhaps, there was slightly less pain in her chest, she would be assailed by a fresh memory. A car like James's on the road ahead of her; someone wearing his cologne as she walked through the shopping centre; the peonies they'd planted bursting into billowing flower without him there to see them. And then she'd fall back into the hole of grief again, as if all the progress she'd made had been nothing but fantasy. It was as if James had just died yesterday, instead of it being over a year now.

'Sheila's never been to Paris, I'm sure of that,' Hettie was saying thoughtfully. 'She left Ireland forty years ago for the US and she's only been back six or seven times, so I don't think the rest of Europe figured much in her plans. Her mother used to suck her in like a Venus Flytrap and not let her go anywhere when she came home. This time I've told her that she can't spend the whole time in the nursing home with her mother. Lord knows, her mother won't know her from Adam, and only hideous guilt would keep her there every day. No point in beating yourself up about life,' Hettie added. 'Life beats us up enough as it is.'

Hettie took down Emily's kitchen calendar, which had almost nothing written on it any more, apart from reminders about bin-recycling day. It was a gardener's calendar because Emily and James had adored their garden and used to spend hours in it, weeding, pruning, deadheading. But not any more. The garden was where she and James had shared so many hours. Now the flower beds were a mess and the vegetable patch was a jungle. Emily couldn't bear to look out of the kitchen window, never mind go outside and see how wild everything had become.

'The third weekend of Sheila's holiday is your anniversary,' Hettie murmured. 'We'll fly to Paris on Thursday and come home on Tuesday.'

'I don't want to go,' said Emily. 'Go to Paris on my wedding anniversary when my husband is dead? The children will think I've lost my mind.'

'Carrie and Mike will be delirious that you're doing something instead of sitting home dying a little every day,' said Hettie firmly. 'Do it for them.'

Emily glared at her sister.

'That was a cheap trick,' she said.

'But you're coming, aren't you?' Hettie asked with a hint of a satisfied smile.

She could barely remember Sheila, who'd been Hettie's best friend in school. Emily had been seven years younger, and all she could recall was a tall girl who was certainly Hettie's partner in naughtiness. Hettie was vague about the modern Sheila, who was recently divorced and liked to knit.

'Never goes anywhere without her knitting,' Hettie said, summoning up a picture for Emily of a gentle soul who found comfort in crafts.

At the airport, Hettie's two giant suitcases made Emily realise that Hettie and Sheila were clearly soul sisters in the kitchen-sink school of packing. Clad in a zebra-print wrap dress straining at the bosom, Sheila wore high red shoes, had bouffant, pearly-blonde hair and moved in a cloud of Opium. Emily's first thought was that Sheila didn't look like much of a knitter. In a heartbeat, she found herself engulfed in zebra print, bosom and wafts of perfume as Sheila hugged her and muttered: 'You poor lamb. A good holiday is what you need.'

On the plane, it became apparent why Hettie and Sheila had gone down in the convent annals as naughty monkeys. Together they were dynamite. Sheila bought Toblerones from duty-free, and once they had a few gin and tonics inside them on the plane (much gin, little tonic), they appeared to regress to their teenage years and talked loudly about past dates as they noisily crunched chocolate.

'George! You must be kidding. I never liked him. He was a total groper!' insisted Hettie loudly. 'Hands everywhere, like an octopus.'

'He was a nice tennis player,' Sheila said.

'Only so he could look up short tennis skirts!'

They were off again, roaring, laughing loudly.

Emily wondered if the reason their section of the plane was so quiet was because everyone was eavesdropping on Hettie and Sheila's conversation.

Their hotel was in the 5th Arrondissement, a picture-postcard vision of Parisian beauty discreetly tucked away on a small street. Alone, Emily thought how James would have liked this pretty room and the walled garden it overlooked. She opened the double doors on to a tiny iron balcony and looked properly into the garden. Someone had designed it beautifully, with a small rose section to the front and secluded paths around beautiful foliage to the rear. The autumnal colours of the leaves were wet with faint drizzle, and they seemed to gleam to Emily's eye.

James would have instantly wanted to see the garden.

'Come on, Em, let's see what they've got.'

Hettie and Sheila had other plans. They wanted dinner and a show.

'The Moulin Rouge!' breathed Sheila.

Dinner involved much heavy flirting from Sheila with the waiters, who flirted back.

'I'm in love,' she sighed, when her favourite whisked away her plate of moules. 'Look at his bum in those trousers.'

Hettie and Emily dutifully looked.

'Sheila, you're in the sort of love that comes with half a bottle of red wine and a Dubonnet,' giggled Hettie, and they were off again.

'Bet you he's wearing Marks 'n' Sparks bum-lifting tights under those trousers,' said Emily, and clapped a hand over her mouth when she realised she'd made a joke, a risqué one at that. And the ceiling hadn't collapsed under the weight of heavenly disapproval of a widow having a laugh.

'Bet you he has!' squealed Sheila.

'You'd rupture yourself getting them off!' roared Hettie, who was laughing so hard she had to hold on to her stomach.

And suddenly Emily was joining in, laughing at the ridiculousness of it all – an ardent Sheila and the young waiter trying to get his tights off. She laughed until her ribs hurt, and it was wonderful.

'You want the dessert menu?' asked the waiter, returning, and if he wondered why the three ladies were struggling to contain their mirth, he said nothing. Probably used to mad women coming to Paris and losing their marbles, Emily thought, wiping her eyes with her napkin.

The Moulin Rouge was not entirely what they'd expected: totally jammed, very expensive and nothing more outrageous than tall showgirls showing lots of boob onstage.

'Is that it?' demanded Hettie. 'Is this the sort of hedonistic carry-on that Sister Patricia in school warned us against? Other women's boobs, and men pie-eyed staring at them?'

'Mine are better, no doubt about it,' said Sheila, having a look down her expansive and impressive cleavage. 'See?'

She was pulling her deep V-necked dress down to look, and several other patrons of the establishment were smiling at her and raising their glasses.

'I'd say you could do a turn onstage if you asked,' said Hettie, giggling.

'You'd look fabulous in one of those cancan outfits,' Emily said, joining in. 'Or the feathery headpieces and six-inch heels!'

And they were off again, laughing.

'Come on,' said Hettie, 'let's go. We're feminists, ladies. We can look in the mirror if we want to see breasts. And I could kill for a cup of tea back at the hotel.'

In their hotel room, Hettie and Sheila switched on a travel kettle and produced teabags, powdered milk, sugar and custard creams for their late-night snack, but Emily said she'd join them in a few minutes.

'There's something I want to do first,' she said.

In her own room, she discovered that she'd put James's old gardening waxed jacket in her suitcase instead of her own. She put it on, its heaviness like having his arm over her shoulders. She could smell his cologne on it, and in one of the pockets was a list he'd made about moving the Japanese maple to the other side of their garden.

Her fingers clutched around the list, she made her way downstairs and found the door to the garden. There was a veranda area, shaded from the rain and with little iron tables for people to enjoy their café au lait.

There was nobody there in the moonlight but Emily. She began to walk around the garden, breathing in the scent of wet earth mixed with leaves – James's favourite scent, he always said. She reached out to touch the bark of a gnarled old fig tree in a secluded corner. James had always wanted one, but the climate was too cool for fig trees.

'You'd love this one, James,' she said aloud. 'Perhaps I should plant one anyway. And move the Japanese maple.'

He'd hate to see their own garden now. A jungle,

when he'd worked so hard on it. She owed it to him to tidy it all up. And she owed it to herself. Tomorrow morning, she'd take her notebook into the walled garden and make some notes, see if she could get any new hints for the garden at home. She and James had worked so hard on it, all that love couldn't go to waste.

And then she'd accompany Sheila and Hettie on their next manic trip out. Paris was special, after all. Upstairs, there was more fun waiting and a cup of tea with her name on it.

The Scrapbook

BY ERIN KELLY

'*H*ow do I look?' Amanda checked her hair in the passenger mirror again. The black skirt that had been on the knee in her wardrobe mirror had ridden up to expose a few inches of thigh. Were her legs still good enough to carry it off?

'You look great, Mum,' said Heidi, turning into the little cobbled mews. They pulled up outside Gordon's Bar.

The man she was meeting – she still only knew him by his online profile name, Teddy_1964 – had let her choose the venue, and she'd opted for Gordon's because the lights were low, the jazz was soft and the wine list expensive enough to keep the kids out. Now she was here, Amanda wanted to stay in the car.

'Oh God, I can't,' she said. 'I'm too nervous. It's been twenty years since I did anything like this.'

'Just be yourself,' said Heidi. 'Just relax and enjoy it.'

Only a teenager could be so casual. Heidi might have understood that it was time for Amanda to move on, might have even helped her set up her online dating profile, but there were some things even the most mature eighteen-year-old could never grasp. Such as what it was like to go on your first blind date in your forties. Such as how it felt wearing matching underwear for the first time in a decade.

'I'll try,' she promised, then took a deep breath and got out of the car.

It took her eyes a while to adjust to the cavernous interior of Gordon's, where the only light came from candles on the tables. How would she recognise Teddy_1964? Like her, he'd only posted an arty, blurry portrait of himself on the dating site. She was still peering into the darkness when a voice behind her called out her own online name.

'MsMandarin?' he said softly, and then, 'Mandy?'

Amanda froze. It was a long time since she had let anyone call her Mandy. She knew that voice. It was gravelled with time, but there was no mistaking it. Slowly, she turned to face him and watched his recognition mirror her own.

'Mandy? I don't believe it!'

'Edward?' she said, in a voice that cracked with disbelief.

'Teddy_1964 to you,' he said. 'Talk about coincidence. Let me look at you.'

He leaped up from his seat in the booth and held her by her upper arms, his gaze sweeping her up and down. His eyes did not suggest that he disapproved of the skirt. Quite the opposite, in fact. Amanda hoped it was dark enough to cover the blush that stained her cheeks.

'My God, Mandy. You look stunning.'

He didn't look so bad himself. The crinkles around his eyes had become grooves, and his hair was more silver than black. Both these things suited him.

'What are the odds . . . ?' Amanda began.

'It must be, what, twenty years?' he replied.

Twenty-one, thought Amanda.

Twenty-one since she'd last seen him on the platform at Oxford railway station, his receding figure blurred by her tears. Theirs had been a sixth-form romance that had not survived the first term at university.

'Mandy,' he'd said. 'I'm so sorry, but I think I've met someone new.'

She'd been too shocked to speak, let alone to fight for him, to show him that whatever he had with this new girl from his law course, it couldn't touch what they had together. The rebound affair with Pete – dull, dependable Pete – had been unplanned, as had the pregnancy that eventually became Sam. She'd still heard about Edward from time to time, but by the time Heidi was born a few years later, they had lost touch altogether.

But now here he was, opposite her, pouring her a glass of Merlot and looking as nervous as she felt.

'So, what have you been up to for the last two decades?' he asked.

'Oh, you know,' she said. 'Marriage. Kids. Divorce. Work. I teach ceramics at what used to be the polytechnic. How about you?'

'Nothing that creative, I'm afraid. I sold my soul and

stuck with law. My ex is Spanish, and I lived in Madrid for a long time. After the split, I wanted to come home again. My kids are at uni, and my firm's opening up a branch here, and my parents aren't getting any younger, so . . . here I am.'

They lifted their glasses at the same time, caught each other's eye and smiled.

'How long have you been single?'

'Six months,' said Amanda.

He winced in sympathy.

'Still raw?' he asked.

'Oh, I'm fine. It was all quite amicable and civilised, really. We just sort of drifted further and further apart, until one day . . .'

'It's funny how time changes you,' said Edward. 'Or maybe it doesn't change you enough, maybe that's the problem.'

They reminisced about the old days, and the music they had loved together. But as the night wore on, it became apparent that they had new things in common now, too: the shock of seeing your children become young adults, and the knowledge of what that meant for you. The frustration of email, and how they missed record shops and letters but were terrified to say so in case it made them sound old.

'I thought about you over the years, you know.'

His face flashed with something that might have been regret, then he brightened.

'Hey – do you remember the scrapbook?'

'That old thing,' she said, trying to keep her voice light.

How could she forget?

The scrapbook hadn't been anything special to the naked eye – just a cheap brown thing, one of a pack of three from Woolworth's or somewhere – but together they had turned it into something amazing. Anything and everything that reminded them of their relationship they had kept and gummed into its pages. Polaroids taken at parties by friends. Ticket stubs from the gigs they'd been to together. Receipts from meals in cheap Italian restaurants where they hadn't noticed that the wine was corked and the pasta was half cooked and the waiters were rolling their eyes and stacking tables on the chairs around them. Edward had gone through the local paper and cut out pictures of houses for sale on the local millionaire's row, big expensive mansions that they would live in when they were married, and fill with children.

'I wonder what happened to it?' he sighed.

'I wonder,' said Amanda. Suddenly tears were pushing at her eyes and there was a stone in her throat. She didn't trust herself to speak. Edward took her hand across the table and traced circles on her palm with his thumb.

'I'd like to take you out again,' he said. 'Same place, tomorrow night?'

She was torn between what her head was telling her to do and the effect of his skin on hers again.

'Could we make it Friday?' she asked, knowing that

Heidi was going up to London to stay with Sam for the weekend, and that she would have the house to herself.

'I'd love that,' he said. 'But don't make me wait any longer. God, of all the luck, of all the random chances . . .'

On the way out, she took a coaster with the Gordon's logo on it and put it in her pocket. He hailed her a cab before finding one for himself. When he kissed her goodbye, the years fell away.

Friday passed in a blur of nerves and excitement. She was so nervous that she shaved the same leg twice, and had to take a last-minute shower to do the other one. While she waited for her taxi, she double-checked that the house was presentable, closing the door on Heidi's heap of a bedroom and locking up the study. The sitting room worried her. Was it too mumsy, with its patchwork throws and home-made pottery? Edward made her feel sexy and glamorous again, and she wanted her home to reflect that. She took down from a high shelf the vinyl she hadn't played in years and stacked it by the hi-fi, and piled the logs in the hearth ready for a romantic fire.

Gordon's was always busy at the weekend, but Edward had bagged their booth again.

'Of all the bars, in all the towns, in all the world, she walks into mine,' he said, holding his arms out to her. This time, they did not sit opposite each other but shared a bench and snogged like teenagers. They didn't get as far as ordering food. Their taxi – just one, this time – was called for half past nine.

As it was, they saw nothing of the sitting room. They were through the door and upstairs within seconds. Amanda left the lights on and didn't care.

Afterwards, he fell asleep in her arms the way he always used to. She'd forgotten about that. She lay next to him, feeling the rise and fall of his chest.

Eventually, when she was sure that Edward was asleep, she tiptoed across the hall and into her study, got her camera from the drawer beside the desk and stole back into the bedroom. She turned the dimmer switch up slowly, so as not to wake him. Checking the flash was off and the sound was muted, she took a snapshot of him.

Back in the study, she printed off the photograph she'd just taken and waved it in the air to dry. Checking again that she'd locked the door behind her, she opened her filing cabinet and took from the top drawer a pile of scrapbooks, numbered one to three. Volume One was the tattiest, most weathered of the books, stuffed with fading Polaroids, gig programmes, passport photos, love notes, promises, hopes and dreams. The last page contained a train ticket to Oxford that was curling at the edges. The last four pages were empty.

Volume Two was pasted with newspaper cuttings about Edward's career, from the various legal journals she used to subscribe to just to feel closer to him. There were pages of photographs she'd taken of him through the window sharing Christmas dinner with his parents at the old house, and others taken of him jogging around the old town. More recently, there were computer printouts of the Facebook account with the slack privacy settings that meant anyone could view his profile. She had wanted to frame the status update from the day he announced his divorce on his Timeline. Purely coincidentally, this was also the day she'd told Pete that it was over between them. Then there was the list of things he'd bought and sold on eBay, where his account name was Teddy_1964. That had been the breakthrough, the clue that had led her straight to the profile on the dating website.

Volume Three was empty. Amanda spread the back of her photograph with glue and stuck it at the bottom of the first page, directly underneath the Gordon's coaster. The tatty old book finally had its destiny fulfilled; the first chapter of the rest of their relationship had begun. She stowed the scrapbooks in the filing cabinet and locked the study door. She turned the dimmer switch back down. In the dark, she pressed herself into Edward's back and smiled.

The Scent of Night

BY DEBORAH LAWRENSON

*T*he sun cut sharp as a blade across the floor tiles. Penny felt the warmth on her face as she padded to the window and pushed open the wooden shutters to embrace the morning. Beyond the courtyard and the garden below, the wide blue ripples of the Luberon hills hung like a great curtain across the landscape.

The only sounds came from the first sleepy cicadas. Perfection: the beauty and peace of a month in Provence; the summer heat and light. The rambling farmhouse they had rented hadn't disappointed, far from it. Inside and out, there was space to breathe and long, calming views from the hillside. Trees whispered in the cooling breezes. Sunk into the garden was a swimming pool with water the colour of glacier melt.

'Are you going down to get the bread, or am I?' John's voice carried a plea, a hung-over-sounding appeal to her good nature. He was still a sheeted walrus on the bed.

'It's your turn,' said Penny. 'And they're your guests.'

And I wish they'd go, she thought. Not even in the

sense of 'leave', just go to the boulangerie one morning for once, instead of expecting to be waited on as if they were staying in a hotel. Because this holiday was supposed to be their anniversary treat (twenty-five years married!), but it hadn't quite been the paradise she'd hoped for.

It had been fun while Sam and Lottie were staying, but they were adults now, with jobs and commitments of their own, and plans that didn't include spending too much time with Mum and Dad. After the children, their partners and assorted friends had gone, Penny and John had a huge, empty house in the South of France to themselves. That was fine with Penny. She had visions of sitting in the shady courtyard under a fragrant fig tree and reading, or wandering around gorgeous villages looking at *brocante* markets and drinking glasses of light, fruity rosé at lunchtime, all the things she never seemed to have time to do at home, what with working part-time and volunteering at the Citizens Advice Bureau.

But it hadn't worked out like that.

Instead of drifting dreamily around lavender fields and spending long, lazy afternoons doing whatever we want, Penny thought, as she scooped up the car keys and her straw basket for the bread and croissants, I have been running a small hotel and restaurant for all the friends and family John invited to drop by as it seemed a shame not to make the most of it. It was amazing how many of them had taken him up on the offer.

And now, after three weeks of hot-flush-fuelled cooking and cleaning and bed-making, John's old workmate Simon was the final straw. He had turned up, newly divorced, with a younger woman in tow – and she was awful. Her name was Sassy, short for Saskia. She was a pin-slim, groomed corporate lawyer in her early thirties and she lay by the pool all day checking her BlackBerry. And it went without saying she never lifted a finger to help, and looked with pity at Penny and the cellulite that no sarong could mask – though not enough pity actually to get dressed and volunteer to do the supermarket run for a change, of course.

She was waiting for Penny downstairs, a vision of blonde good health in a wisp of beachwear.

'Are you going into town?' she asked. 'Because if you are, could you get me some more suncream?'

Saskia studied one slim, bronzed arm. 'Factor fifteen ought to do it.'

Penny opened her mouth to suggest that perhaps Sassy might like to go herself, as the chemist was only a few doors away from the bread shop, but closed it again as she realised that left to Sassy, there would probably be no breakfast. She seemed to exist on hot water and slices of lemon.

'Who owns this place, again?' asked Sassy.

Penny had the impression their guest had had a good nose around while she was alone downstairs.

'A composer and his wife.'

'It's all a bit of a mishmash, isn't it?'

'I rather like it,' Penny said, beginning to walk off. She supposed some of the old French furniture had seen better days. The large, splashy paintings on the walls were flaking. And the brown wood statue of a monk in the hall was a little unsettling, as was the wall sconce of an arm reaching out of the iron frame with a candle. But it was shabby chic, wasn't it? It was perfect for this house of white walls speckled with the patina of time and gleaming terracotta tiles on the floors, as were the rusty garden chairs and odd stone artefacts outside.

Anyway, Penny thought but didn't say, if this doesn't suit you, go somewhere else. But after three days, Sassy and Simon showed no signs of moving on.

Later that morning, Penny had returned with the supplies (and the suncream, which Sassy had just picked up from the kitchen island and hadn't even offered to pay for), and was making a cheesecake for dinner. She absent-mindedly licked the mixing spoon, then started to scrape the bowl. She felt fat and dragged down. It is a truth universally acknowledged (though not nearly often enough), thought Penny, that a woman approaching fifty is in need of a husband who likes a good armful because, by God, that was what he'd be getting.

Through the kitchen window she noticed that Sassy had taken her bikini top off. John – straining to hold his stomach in – was eagerly adjusting the parasol above her and taking his time about it, while Simon handed her a drink. Unless he leaves me for a younger model, of course, Penny hastily revised her homely assumption. He was still a good-looking man, big and broad with a lovely, generous nature. A younger woman would be lucky to have him.

The drinking went on throughout the lunch Penny laid out on the terrace: a vibrant tomato salad on a deep cobalt-blue plate; goat's cheese and sweet onion tartlets; pâté and fresh bread. The sun seared down from the bluest of skies. When everyone else had slunk off for a siesta, a sober Penny cleared the dishes away, made herself a cup of coffee and went down to the pool with her book. She tipped her face up to the heat, luxuriating in the time alone.

That evening, the sunset burned rosy tangerine streaked with gold. Everyone assembled expectantly by the table on the terrace. Penny produced more chilled wine and a sumptuous dinner, and repeated the catering process. Sassy only picked at the sea bream and ribbons of courgette. She was comfortably installed on a cushioned chair, telling the men about the high-profile cases she had worked on, making them laugh and admire her even more with tales of defeated opposition and great men brought down, as Penny got up and cleared away. In the kitchen, she cut herself a hefty misery slice of cheesecake as she surveyed the stacks of plates. A light tinkling of laughter from Sassy wafted through to the kitchen. Penny drowned her out by crashing pans loudly, but no one seemed to notice.

After midnight, Penny lay in bed unable to drop off

to sleep. Next to her, John started to snore gently. The trouble was, Penny thought, I'm on my own with this. I am just myself, and Sassy is an invincible career woman and yoga-toned sex goddess. She tried not to think about what was going on in the bedroom down the corridor. But all that success shouldn't stop her from behaving with basic courtesy, even if friendliness was too much to hope for.

Perhaps a fellow Grumpy Old Woman might have noticed Sassy's selfishness, but the men wouldn't have a clue. And in comparison, there was no doubt about it: Penny had let herself go. She was wondering rather reluctantly whether she might have to start going to some kind of gym, when she gradually became aware of a scent carried on the air. It was a lovely perfume of vanilla and sweet lavender, which then became a kind of chocolate smoke. Minute by minute it was becoming stronger, until it seemed to pervade the room.

It was either coming through the open window from outside, from some night-fragrant plant down in the courtyard – or was it from a scented candle that Sassy had lit? Penny got out of bed and went out on to the terrace outside the bedroom and breathed in deeply. The scent was carried off by a faint breath of wind in the dark. Above was a luminous arc of silver stars, bright and burning in the black sky. All was still and quiet.

It was strange; the scent didn't seem to be coming from the garden. Penny waited a while, enjoying the profound silence, then went back to bed. In the dark-ness, she lay on her back enveloped by the aroma from a source that was still mysterious and closed her eyes.

But when she mentioned it the next day, Sassy didn't know what Penny was talking about.

'I can assure you it was nothing to do with me,' she insisted.

'It was pungent – lavender and rose and vanilla and chocolate and burnt almonds. Really strong and smoky. I was wondering if it was a candle, or something . . .' persisted Penny.

But Sassy shook her head and denied everything. 'I only ever wear a very light, delicate perfume. I absolutely loathe anything strong and smoky. The very thought gives me a headache and makes me want to run.'

That evening, at Simon's suggestion, they went out to a restaurant on the edge of a beautiful hilltop village. Penny had put on a new maxi dress and pulled herself together. She took a little more time and trouble with her make-up, and decided that whatever happened she would make an effort. It was so lovely to be taken out to eat this evening, instead of taken for granted.

From their table outside, under a vine canopy, they could see for miles. All down the valley, the distinctive vertical crevices in the ridge of the mountain darkened as the air softened until they seemed to be great dusky rivers cascading down to the valley floor.

'To Penny,' said Simon, raising his glass, 'who has looked after us so beautifully. Very much appreciated.'

It was so unexpected, Penny forgot any lingering annoyance. Candles were lit, and dishes of mouth-watering Provençal food arrived. Under the table, John squeezed her hand. Penny felt herself relax in the warm glow of the evening and the effects of the wine, and let Sassy be the centre of attention.

They all drank too much. Simon constantly leaned back in his seat and ordered fresh bottles of palest rosé. Penny, sitting next to him, noticed the criss-cross patterns of red veins in his cheeks, and the way he looked at Sassy as if he couldn't believe his luck that she was with him.

Everyone except Sassy finished with a trio each of crèmes brûlées infused with lavender, thyme and peach. Penny sat back, replete and sleepy. This was the life. But when the bill came and Simon tried to pay, his credit card was refused and it was John who settled up.

Back at the house, another bottle was freed from John's stock.

'Push on through, eh?' roared Simon, pulling the cork.

'I'm going to bed,' said Penny. She didn't want so much as another sip. She heard Sassy coming up about half an hour later, but the men stayed up into the early hours, drinking in the garden.

The next morning, though the sky was cloudless again and the heat rising, there was a distinct chill in the atmosphere. Sassy was fuming.

'We are leaving, as soon as we can,' she hissed as they came downstairs.

Simon blanched. It was clear from her tone that she expected to get her own way.

'And as for you,' she said to Penny, though barely acknowledging her with a glance, 'drenching our room with that suffocating scent after I'd specifically said I can only tolerate the lightest of fragrances . . . It gave me the most appalling night, made me physically sick. I can't think why you did that.'

'But I didn't—'

Sassy waved her words away imperiously. 'You obviously don't want us here, so we're leaving, and that's that.'

Penny decided to offer no resistance.

An hour later, they were saying goodbye, Simon reluctantly and apologetically, struggling with the bags. Sassy strode ahead towards Penny, but the four-inch heels she'd put on for travelling caught on an uneven paving stone as she approached, throwing her towards Penny rather more intimately than either would have liked. They pulled apart awkwardly and exchanged thin smiles. She smelled of lemon pith, sharp and bitter.

'Bye, then,' said Penny.

'Was it you?' asked John. He didn't seem concerned in the slightest.

'No, it wasn't! I didn't go near their room, not since I delivered the fresh towels Sassy asked for, but that was yesterday morning.'

She wondered whether to mention the mysterious perfume, but then John said: 'Poor old Simon.'

'What?' Poor old Simon, the successful entrepreneur with the stunning younger woman? Had her hearing gone, now?

John was positively jaunty as he measured out coffee. 'He poured it all out last night. He's pining for his ex-wife, and he's taken a massive loss on his last deal. There's not much left, and no doubt when Sassy finds out, she'll be off permanently. I know her sort.'

'I thought you thought she was marvellous,' said Penny.

'I was being nice, for Simon's sake. He hasn't had much luck lately.'

Penny sat down with relief. 'She was so irritating,' she said.

'Not a woman of substance,' smiled John, reaching out for her.

'Like me,' she said sadly.

John bent his head and kissed her gently. 'In all the best ways.'

'Three whole days left to ourselves,' said Penny happily.

She pottered into the sitting room and noticed a book had fallen off a shelf. It was an illustrated history of lavender-growing, and she opened it instead of putting it straight back. The first picture was a photograph of a house, this very house. A piece of paper covered in handwritten notes fluttered out.

'Marthe Lincel, creator of perfumes,' Penny read,

'was inspired by her childhood home, Les Genévriers. Lavande de Nuit, her most famous fragrance, was said to capture the spirit of Provence . . .'

Penny took the book outside and spent the whole day reading in the garden. The tranquillity and the books she dipped into were balm for her soul.

That night, she woke and smelled the perfume again. It was a soft, warm caress all around her, and it was heavenly.

The Wedding Day

BY KATHY LETTE

Inspired by Charles Dickens' bicentenary

*H*e arrived in the cobbled courtyard with a sputtering of coachmen and a fusillade of horses' hooves. The other guests swept back like a tide to make way for him to enter the ballroom. The gentleman down from London gave off a rich, dark glow that made everyone around him seem faded. The women stopped dancing and stood in a row like painted ninepins. It didn't take him long to bowl them over. I kept on twirling and whirling from man to man, all the time aware of him watching me. I could feel his gaze like a breath on the nape of my neck.

'You must be the poor orphan girl.' His voice looped across the room and pulled me towards him. 'Marooned on the moors with your gaoler.'

His voice lowered as his eyes flicked towards my spinster aunt, my guardian, skinny-black as a pencil, scrawling disapproval in the air.

'Poor? No, sir. You are mistaken. I am a woman of independent means. As soon as I come of age.' I

159

glanced up from under arched brows into eyes the dazzling colour of a cloudless blue sky. The mysterious gentleman had high cheekbones and a low laugh, and there was a mutinous expression on his handsome face.

'It is a truth universally acknowledged that a single woman in possession of a good fortune must be in want of a husband.'

'The suitors who would win parental imprimatur,' I gestured towards my guardian, 'are sensible, straight-backed . . . and as boring as suet pudding.'

My eyes swept over him, assessing what I saw. My only serious flirtations had been a brief correspondence with the vicar's brother, who laughed too loudly, and a prolonged misunderstanding with a cousin who wrote questionable poetry. This gentleman was far more exotic fare – flashy, fierce, with dancing eyes and a mischievous mouth.

'It seems to me, sir, that married women become either as plump and dull as a cushion. Or reek of disappointment. Having entered the matrimonial fortress, like a medieval village they just crumble away behind its ramparts.'

The stranger gave a rich chuckle. 'I thought young ladies of breeding weren't allowed to read novels. So, Jane Austen was right then. The fair sex has unfair options. Domestic work, governessing . . .'

'Prostitution or marriage. Which is often a tautology,' I fired back. 'For women, wedlock is little more than a padlock.'

Intrigued, the gentleman lifted his eyebrows a

fraction. 'But if you married the right person, the prison would be so pleasurable you would not want to go over the wall.'

The air crackled between us. I felt all at sea, as mystified as the first time I'd seen a picture of hieroglyphics. And yet, in truth, I lived in a hieroglyphic world where people's real feelings were never uttered, only occasionally signalled by a set of arbitrary signs. But here was this hot-blooded man, talking frankly and not about trifles and trivialities. Meeting him was like hearing a cherished note of music I could recognise but not name. It took the fine-tuning of every muscle in my body to keep my face impassive.

'I was worried that fraternising with you coy country girls would be like baiting a field mouse. But you, my dear, have a fine, ferocious heart.'

I felt myself flush and tremble. Other courtiers have tended to drip uxorious sentiment, molasses-like, into my ear. I tried to arrange my expression into something more detached, but he glimpsed my curiosity and my cravings, and his smile curved up at one corner of his full red lips.

My guardian called my name, quickening her step as if to ward off some impending danger.

'How do you do?' she said to the city gentleman. Her voice had a peculiar, ventriloquial quality. Her facial muscles twitched as if a smile were trying to climb on to her face like an insect.

As she briskly escorted me to the waiting coach, her

faint smile narrowed between twin brackets of disapproval.

'A man of noble birth is far above the likes of you,
young lady.'

With cold-blooded complacency, she tossed earth
into the grave of my young hopes. But I refused to be
smothered alive.

And the very next morning, the man my aunt said
was 'above me' was below my window. He shone there
in the courtyard. I was soon to discover that every room
he entered took its shape from his position in it. At the
appearance of an aristocrat, oh, the grovelling of my
aunt, the 'My Lording', the falling down prostrate of
the servants at his well-heeled feet.

The house my parents left me is grand but aloof-
looking. Since their funerals, it has seemed to me a
vast, ghost-riddled mausoleum, the only sound the
continuous death rattle of the old windows. But no
more. Not when he is here, talking of the glittering
attractions of the New World over the dreary gentility
of the Old. He speaks with a throaty richness, redolent
of the aromatic beans and smoky tobacco flavours of
the Americas. The flavours enter my mouth and make
it water. The fire is laid but not lit, although I'm sure
my emotions are so heated they could make the kind-
ling spark.

Each day he visits, enchanting me with tales of his
adventures until my senses are unnaturally enhanced.
There is something of the earthy tang of the New
World about him, the sharp, spicy perfume of

rollicking oceans, the resinous muskiness of teeming forests, the warm-scented winds of pirate isles.

Over the weeks, I found myself drawn towards him like a plant in a dark room inclines towards a wedge of light. In his company I became original and vivid, as though my mind had escaped from the narrow confines of nineteenth-century England to the vast, extravagant spaces of the uncharted world. Walking with him on the moors, I found myself laughing a great deal, making many extravagant gestures with my hands. When a skittish wind pulled at my skirt and my ankles were rashly displayed, his teasing expression was replaced by a look of distant, almost sweet abstraction. The first time he touched my arm, I jumped as if something had nipped me, but my heart beat insubordinately.

'We Englishmen are no better than the Ottomans, the way we insist that women subscribe to our doctrines. We let you move about the world liberally enough, with ringlets and pretty bonnets to disguise you instead of veils and yashmaks. But a woman's soul can only be seen by the man who owns her. She is his indentured slave . . . But you, my dear, are a free spirit. An equal to me in all.'

He may be the explorer, but I was suddenly the empress of a new-found land, a land neither Columbus nor Cortés had mapped. Love . . . I heard a new voice speaking to me, not in any language I'd learned at my governess's knee, but in the secret language of the heart. And who could resist his call? Unless I was tied like Odysseus to the mast of some ship, with clay stopping my ears.

When I laughingly kissed his cheek, relief tightened the skin around his temples. Then his face registered an emotion so intense it stopped me mid-speech.

'I've found you at last.' His voice was that of a drowning man, miraculously rescued. By the brook, he took down my hair. It fell to just below where my small, strong waist begins its curve out towards my hips.

'You'd have me be a fallen woman?'

'How can you fall, when I am here to catch you? Will you marry me and be my love?' He was on one knee, eyes alight with bliss.

My face was so effervescent with joy the world must guess my news. My aunt's face presented the opposite countenance. If looks could pulverise, I would have been pâté. 'Out walking, unchaperoned. Your behaviour is not . . . appropriate.' The word held all the glacial, righteous condemnation of a biblical edict.

His marriage proposal generated a gratifying shock.

'Your hand in marriage?' my aunt marvelled. Her ears were like teapot handles and her voice steamed with excitement.

The night of his proposal, I felt the wild, exhilarating terror of losing my moorings. I couldn't sleep, tossing and turning, my nightgown twisting itself round me into a tight, wrinkled husk. At the sound of his voice calling from the garden, every drop of my blood sprang to attention. I ached for him. I longed for him with the whole of my biology. And when I escaped from the house through the garden doors and ran to him in the moonlight, I felt myself quiver against him with desire. My thin shift disclosed my shoulder, which he kissed. The hill's grassy garment stretched like soft cloth over an anatomy of ancient stone. As he lay me down, I looked up into the interlaced limbs of the trees. Entwined there, in the rooty embrace of the old oak, bathed in soft evening light, his touch felt like fine silk threads laid across my skin. Love ran its hands over my body, welcoming it into womanhood.

The date is set. But before we can wed, there is business to be concluded in London. These long weeks he's been away, I've prepared my trousseau, longing for the miraculous comfort of a letter. Our love is dark as a mystery, bright as joy. What I've experienced is the greatest secret of my life, a secret for which I have no rational explanation and can only unburden here in my diary. My beloved's touch whispers away on my skin as I write.

Another week goes by, and still no word arrives from London. The house smells like joy trapped for so long it is beginning to go sour and rancid. The pretty, winding centre staircase now appears to coil upwards like a snake. The countryside lies damp and cold and grey as a graveyard. Even at church, the single, evil tooth in the gargoyle's face seems aimed like a knife at my heart.

I confide here that without him my life would be immured in marble, as cold and hard as a statue. Without him, I'd become parched as a ghost. My world would reek of mouse droppings and mourning ghouls. It would echo like a cave, the feeble candle flame of remembered love only serving to accentuate every shadow. Without him, I would just bury myself beneath the winter of white dust sheets.

When questioned about the impending nuptials, my aunt's face becomes a knot of anxiety. 'He will come,' I tell her stoutly.

My love feels like a sword sheathed in my body, waiting to lash out at anyone who maligns him. We are part of each other's flesh and blood, we reverberate, body and soul.

And now, finally, my wedding day has dawned. The church swells like a throat with the sound of singing. The brass bell is swinging joyously, sending bursts of sound down the valley. The day is anointed with magic. Birdsong seems to erupt from my body, soaring, celebratory. My face in the mirror is naked in its devotion. I close my eyes, anticipating the heaven of his touch.

My bedroom pitches around me like the deck of the rolling ships he has told me about, and upon which we will soon set sail, euphorically, into our glorious future.

Vibrant with hope and lit up with dreams, I am alive with love.

But here's my aunt at the door, all frilly bonnet and vinegar heart. The tiny fjords of the pitiless years have deepened around her eyes and mouth. Her expression has hardened with disappointment into a face stamped on a coin. She is gesturing like a heroine from a Jacobean tragedy. 'There's a letter.' Her voice rises half an octave, losing much of its well-bred intonation in the process. 'From him.' And then she gives a snort of laughter as merciless as a nose-blowing, 'Miss Havisham.'

A Foreign Affair

BY LESLEY LOKKO

*P*eople here talked about the heat as though it were a person, Charlotte McGregor thought to herself, partly in wonderment, partly in irritation.

As though heat – male or female, she hadn't yet worked it out – rose each day, intent only on making life for the expats who had the misfortune to come to Africa as miserable as possible.

'God, it's hot,' the ladies-who-lunched-and-swam at the five-star hotel pools in town exclaimed to each other, only every other minute or so. What on earth did they expect? A few degrees shy of the equator, it was hardly likely to snow. And if it was hard for them – the Italians, Germans and French women with their olive skins, dark hair and perma-tans – what on earth did they think it was like for her, a Scot? A curly redhead, with translucent white skin that freckled at the touch of the sun and pale blue eyes, certainly not meant for these skies?

On her first morning, after the darkened shroud of her overnight flight, she'd woken up, drawn back the curtains in her hotel room and almost howled in pain.

Now she wore her sunglasses to bed. Well, not quite – but she certainly never left the house without them. She'd been here all of three months, and she'd learned how to adapt and adjust herself to her new surroundings just as they'd taught her back in Whitehall.

It was 1984. She was one of a handful of women who'd taken the Foreign Office entrance exam, passed it with flying colours and, after a short stint in Paris, had found herself the embassy press attaché in a former colony, whose geographical position gave it more importance than it truly deserved – or at least, that was the insider view. No matter: she was twenty-six years old, single and in possession of a large, airy house, two servants and a driver to manage – and the heat, of course. Every morning, at seven on the dot precisely, Mustafa would hoot the horn discreetly – two short blasts. She would collect her keys, pick up her bag and walk jauntily down the short path that led to the street. The car, a blue Peugeot 304 (a concession to the francophone majority) with its bright red-and-white diplomatic plates, would be parked directly outside her gate, as though to spare her the extra sweat that a few steps to the left or right would entail.

But where was Mustafa? Charlotte looked at her watch for the third time. It was nearly seven thirty. In three months of Monday-to-Friday he'd never once been late, despite the overheard dire predictions of the ladies-who-lunched-and-swam. 'They're always bloody late. Can't stick to anything, least of all time.' Not Mustafa. She'd always been able to set her watch by him. She drew back the curtains in the dining room and peered out into the lush, tropical garden. Another strange thing: Georges, the elderly gardener from next door, wasn't in his usual spot, raking the driveway to a smooth pebbled finish as his employer, the Swedish ambassador, liked it. And where were the guards? Four of them, interchangeable, with names she'd never learned . . . they stood sentinel day and night, guarding the ambassador – though quite why the Swedish ambassador needed armed, twenty-four-hour protection was anyone's guess. Still, it didn't answer the question: where were they all?

The sounds that carried across the diplomatic quarter where the lawns were kept watered and cut and the electricity seldom went out were confusing at first. A series of dull thumps, like the rolling thunder rumbles, followed immediately by a high-pitched whistle and then a second, deafening thunderclap. She'd never heard anything like it. Once, twice, thrice . . . the sequence continued dully.

She looked at the phone. If something had happened, something untoward . . . but what? She bit her lip uncertainly. If something really had happened, surely someone from the embassy would've phoned? Now another sound was added to the roll call: the whistling, whirring drone of a helicopter overhead. She ignored protocol and ran towards the front door. She yanked it open, forgetting her sunglasses, and turned her face up towards the already blinding sky. There it was, a lone mechanical bird, its rotary wings catching the sun with a ferocious glare, skidding towards the centre of town. Then she saw the thick plume of smoke rising lazily from the spot where she knew the local football ground to be. Something had happened. Something real. Her heart was racing as she tried to recall what to do in such an emergency; what she'd been taught to do.

She ran back inside the house and picked up the phone. Contact your superiors, adhere to the chain of command. But the phone line was dead. She dropped it as though it were hot. She looked around her. The sitting room, with its inoffensive magnolia walls, Danish-style furniture and embassy-issue watercolours of an English landscape she'd never seen, looked back blankly at her. *Whummmmp!* A deep, baritone explosion rocked the house. A sudden movement caught her eye through the open front door. It was Patience, her house help. She ran outside.

'Patience! Oh, thank God . . . what's going on, Patience?' Palms outstretched, appealing. She'd always 'got along' with Patience, unlike Mercy, the older, sullen woman who washed her clothes.

But Patience looked at her with the same blank expression that Mercy usually wore. 'They are fighting,' she said eventually. She was carrying a bag in one hand, one of those blue-and-red striped nylon bags that you saw everywhere.

'Who? Who is fighting?' Charlotte asked, fear beginning to take proper hold. 'Who?' she asked again, wanting to take Patience by the shoulders and shake her.

Patience shrugged. She shifted her weight from one foot to the other, clearly wanting to be off. But where? Charlotte looked around her again. Beyond the garden, the street was completely empty. It was nearly eight a.m. On weekday mornings the street was thick with diplomatic and government cars, ferrying embassy staff and high-ranking state officials from their homes in the shady, leafy part of town once reserved for the former colonial masters. Today nothing stirred, not even the trees. 'You better go, madam.' Patience spoke slowly. She shouldered her bag and started towards the gate.

'But where?'

Patience didn't reply. The gate opened and closed behind her. Somewhere, further down the street, Charlotte heard an engine start. Someone had obviously come for Patience, but what about her? She ran down to the gate, holding on to it, looking up and down the street in both directions, white-knuckled. Her passport; she ought to run and get her passport. There were spirals of grey and white smoke everywhere now, and there was more than one helicopter slicing its way through the sky.

Eight seventeen a.m., and still there wasn't a person outside. She looked at the houses on either side of her; curtains still drawn as though the flimsy net could provide the same level of protection that the guards outside once had. Should she run to one of them?

She'd met the Swedish ambassador once or twice at the mundane cocktail parties at which people of their kind met. Across the way was someone from the Food and Agriculture Organisation – Italian, or Spanish, she couldn't remember.

She'd only been here three months. Her closest colleagues were at least three streets away – the Cunninghams, John and Rita. John was the head of Consular Services. He'd know what to do, surely . . . but did she dare walk out into the streets to get to them? Two fighter jets screamed overhead, releasing something that fell, fell, fell . . . and then exploded dully, somewhere close to the airport. There was nothing for it. She ought to run. She had to run. For her life. She grabbed her handbag, making sure her passport was safely in it, and ran out of the house. The street was almost empty but at the end of it, just where it hit the main road, she could see people running towards something – or away, she couldn't yet tell. She shouldered her bag and ran on.

'Charlotte? Charlotte!' A voice cut across the heaving, swaying, chanting mass of people surging up Independence Avenue towards the central bus station. She swung round wildly. In the middle of the road, in the midst of the grinding, bumping wall of bodies – market mammies with their produce shoved rudely into bags; children holding on to parents, sisters, relatives for dear life; men with picks and shovels; young women with panniers of mangoes and sweets still incongruously balanced on their heads – a car crawled along at a snail's pace. She peered at the face staring at her through the window only a foot or so away.

'Tumi?' She stared at him. Tumi Dumisané had been, of all places, at Fettes in Edinburgh, in the same year as her brother, a fact she'd known even before coming here. Jamie had told her as soon as she'd received her posting. 'Look out for Tumi. He's a good guy. One of the few.' A few years older than her, he was in government; one of the President's senior policy advisors. They met intermittently at the same cocktail parties where she'd met her neighbours; he lived with his wife and children several streets down from her. He jogged past her house sometimes in the predawn coolness.

'Get in!' He reached behind him and thrust the back door violently open. 'Get in!'

She clambered in without even thinking. 'What's going on?' she asked, realising as she spoke that her teeth were chattering. She was sitting behind him; the car – a plain, nondescript Japanese car, not the usual dark blue Mercedes in which he was driven – was empty.

His eyes met hers in the rear-view mirror. 'A coup d'état. Junior officers. The worst kind.'

Charlotte swallowed. She'd forgotten everything she'd been told about what to do in the event of a coup. 'Wh-where are you going?' she stammered. Her hands were gripping the steel poles of his headrest.

'My grandmother's place. It's on the other side of

town. No one will think to look for anyone important there.' That she too was to be included was unspoken.

Four days, three nights – the longest and most passionate of her life. It was there, in one of the oldest and most densely crowded parts of town that her daughter, Cassie, was conceived. Not that Cassie – or Tumi, for that matter – would ever know it. After four days, Charlotte McGregor was one of the lucky foreigners delivered up to the US Marines who'd come to save them. Others were not so lucky.

15 June 2013

Charlotte McGregor, the Mayor's right-hand woman and the one through whom all must pass, is waiting by the front doors. She's an attractive woman in her early fifties, tall and slim with short, close-cropped dark hair and a pair of stylish, black-framed glasses that hide her pale blue eyes. She's something of an enigma to her colleagues; she keeps herself to herself, and although she's been at the Mayor's side for nearly twenty years, not much is known about her or her personal life. She has a daughter, Cassie, who's at drama school, a vivacious, dark-skinned girl with a shock of thick, curly hair . . . lots of speculation there, of course, but few have ever asked – who's the father?

The delegation from the small African country few at City Hall could locate on a map is almost upon them. It's the last few days of London's bid for the

Commonwealth Games, and the political horse-trading is intense. There are many who feel London's had more than her fair share of world events, and the Mayor is throwing a lavish reception for those few countries whose votes might still be swayed. As the officials from both sides troop noisily into the hall, Charlotte extends a hand and gives a professional handshake, accompanied by a warm smile. 'Welcome to London, sir. Welcome to the Mayor's office.' She repeats it again and again, discreetly consulting the list in her hand so that she knows who's who.

'Charlotte.'

She looks up. The cool shock of recognition sweeps through her like a wave. 'Tumi.' She blinks slowly. Her eyes go back down to the list in her hand. She frowns at it uncomprehendingly. 'You weren't on the list,' she says stupidly, at last.

He smiles. 'I'm never on the list. I wasn't then, I'm not now.' The voice is still the same; low, confidential, infinitely appealing. He touches her lightly on the elbow. 'Have a drink with me. Later. You look well, by the way,' he says, as he's swept away in the official crowd. 'Very well.'

She gazes after him, too surprised to speak. A pleasurable warmth spreads slowly through her. Tumi Dumisané. After all these years. She puts up a hand to the only jewellery she ever wears aside from the stylish, chunky silver rings, of which she has many.

Around her neck she's always worn a thin, delicate gold locket. Over the years, the photo inside has been replaced several times. It's Cassie, now twenty-eight, nearly the same age as Charlotte was when she spent four days huddled in a darkened room in a part of a town she'd once lived in and hadn't even known existed.

She'll show it to him, of course. She touches the locket lightly. She looks over at him, now chatting easily with the Mayor, who already seems utterly smitten. Tumi Dumisané. She smiles suddenly, surprising the colleague who's standing next to her. He's never seen a smile like it on her before. 'Excuse me,' she says quickly, moving away. She walks towards the bar and picks up two flutes of champagne.

Later is now.

Let's be Honest

BY JILL MANSELL

*M*el first saw him as she was making her way home through the cemetery. Dark-haired, quite handsome but not startlingly so, and sad. Oh goodness, but there was just something about him that made her think, He's nice; if I knew him I'd like him, I'm sure.

The next morning, on her way to work, she paused beside the grave he'd been visiting. *Suzannah, aged 33, beloved wife of James* – those were the words carved into the white marble headstone. She'd died two years ago. Mel's heart went out to poor James; what a terrible thing to have to go through. No wonder he'd looked so sad.

You know how sometimes you catch sight of someone and can't get them out of your head? Well, this was what had happened with James. All day at work she found herself thinking about him. And that evening, again around six, her heart began to beat extra fast at the sight of him in the cemetery. The sun was still warm, shimmering through the leaves on the trees. He was wearing a pale yellow striped shirt and dark grey suit trousers, and was changing the water in the metal vase containing the exuberant spray of stargazer lilies he'd brought along with him yesterday.

Glancing up as she passed him, he nodded and smiled in that polite way strangers do when their paths cross in a cemetery. And wow, what a smile . . . Mel felt her intestines do a giddy backflip. Maybe moving back to Bristol had been the right thing to do after all.

Flustered and wondering if he was still looking at her, she turned her attention to the graves bordering the pathway. Having run into him two days in a row, might he wonder if she was stalking him? Not that she was, but what if that was what it looked like?

Mel realised she'd slowed down and was staring at a black granite headstone engraved in grey and silver. *Alex Brewster, tragically taken too young, aged 38. Much loved and missed.* She blinked; how had Alex died? Had he been riding his motorbike too fast in driving rain? Could it have been a mountain-climbing accident? Was he a fireman who'd been killed attempting some heroic rescue? Because that was the thing about gravestones; they made you long to know more. What had he looked like, for example? In her mind's eye, Alex Brewster was big and burly with ruffled fair hair and a rugby-player's physique. He had a loud, infectious laugh and maybe a broken nose, too.

Reaching forward, Mel brushed away a couple of dead leaves that had attached themselves to the front of the stone. Alex had died three years ago. Out of the corner of her eye, she saw James glancing over in her direction, and in that split second knew what she needed to do. Fishing a tissue out of her bag, she licked it and stepped forward again in order to wipe away the splatter of white bird poo on the top of the headstone.

'There, that's better.' With a fond smile, she ran her hand over the carved letters that made up Alex's name. 'All clean again.'

The next moment she heard the crunch of gravel underfoot and saw that James was leaving, making his way back to the car park. This time, as he passed behind her, Mel didn't turn around. Instead she patted Alex's headstone and said, 'Bye then, darling. See you tomorrow. I'm going home now.'

The next day was grey and gloomy and James didn't appear, but she left flowers on Alex's grave anyway. They'd had dahlias on offer at half price in the supermarket but, not wanting to seem cheap, she'd gone for the mixed red and orange chrysanthemums instead. They looked gorgeous too, big and bold, brash and cheerful, like Alex himself. It felt a bit odd, admittedly, standing alone at the graveside of someone you didn't know, but why shouldn't he have flowers and a visitor? Didn't everyone enjoy a bit of company, after all?

On Saturday evening, though, James was back, wearing jeans and a white polo shirt and carrying more flowers. Mel smiled and said, 'Hello,' as she passed him on her way to the standpipe, and this time he gave her a proper smile, nodding and saying, 'Hi,' in return.

She hadn't even noticed before that he had the most fetching dimple . . .

The next minute, she'd turned on the tap at the standpipe, accidentally splashing ice-cold water all over her skirt, legs and shoes. Jumping back and letting out a shriek of dismay, she heard him call out behind her, 'Are you all right?'

'Fine, thanks.' Mel turned and gestured helplessly at herself. 'I'm just an idiot, turned the tap on too hard.'

'I know, it's a vicious one. Here.' And now he was heading over, handing her a handkerchief. 'Use this. It's OK, it's clean.'

Oh wow, this is like something out of a film . . .

'Thanks.' When she'd mopped her legs, her skirt and her shoes, she said, 'I'm Mel, by the way.'

'Hello, Mel. I'm James.'

I know you are! And do you have any idea how fantastically attractive you look when you smile?

Aloud, she said, 'Hi, James. Nice to meet you.' Then she held up the sodden handkerchief. 'Can I wash this and give it back next time we run into each other?'

'Whenever. Are you just visiting, or do you live here in Bristol?'

'I moved back from London last week.'

James walked alongside her back to Alex's grave, then nodded at the headstone as she knelt to rearrange the chrysanths. 'Friend of yours?'

He's lost his wife. Obviously he'd rather talk to someone able to empathise. And really, would Alex mind?

Mel said, 'Boyfriend.'

'Right.' He paused, then said, 'And how long were you two together?'

Yikes, good question. How long?

'Two years.'

'Not easy, is it?'

She shook her head. 'No, it isn't.'

'What was he like, then? Alex?'

'He was amazing.'

Mel felt her throat tighten.

'That's Suzannah over there. My wife. She was amazing, too.'

On her knees, facing away from him, Mel discovered she was no longer able to speak. She just nodded.

'Well, I'll leave you to it,' said James. 'Bye. See you around.'

Mel stayed where she was, feeling sick with shame. It had been a ridiculous daydream that had somehow ended up spilling out of her mouth and becoming a reality. She should have told him the truth. Whatever had possessed her to say such a thing?

And it was too late now; he'd gone. Oh Lord, what had she done?

It had been a week now, and she couldn't put it off any longer. The time came when you simply had to man up and admit to your hideous mistake. She'd written a letter to James, explaining everything and apologising profusely, but even that was a cop-out. She needed to say sorry in person in order to truly repent.

And there was no longer any question of secretly fantasising over him, either; the nanosecond he found out what she'd done, he would be utterly shocked and repulsed. She deserved that humiliation, too. It had been a moment of madness, and she'd despised herself ever since.

Anyway, she was here now. It was five thirty, and he should be along soon.

Mel took a deep, shuddery breath in a futile attempt to calm her nerves. She'd never been so scared in her life. The earlier sunshine had disappeared, and ominous dark clouds were now rolling overhead. Which seemed appropriate.

Ten minutes later, the heavens opened and rain began hammering down like gunfire. Mel, already sitting on one of the wooden benches sheltered by the overhanging branches of the yew trees, stayed where she was and waited. Maybe he wouldn't bother coming along today in weather like this.

But the next moment, she saw him making his way along the gravel path, holding a black umbrella and wearing a long dark coat. For the first time her heart sank rather than doing an excited bunny-hop at the sight of him. Now she was going to have to go ahead and admit everything to his face. If it all became too unbearable, she would hand him the letter currently folded in her pocket.

Spotting her, James raised a hand in greeting and came over to the bench.

'Hi! I think you've got the right idea.' Indicating the sky, he said, 'Mind if I join you until it blows over?'

She shifted up to make room for him and took the washed handkerchief from her bag. 'Here you go. Thanks.'

'No problem. And you've ironed it too. I'm impressed.'

Say it now, say it now, go ahead and say it . . .

'Haven't seen you for a few days,' James went on. 'I wondered if you were ill.'

Could he hear her heart hammering inside her ribcage? Right, get on with it, the rain's stopping. Shaking her head, Mel braced herself to begin. 'No, not ill.'

'Good, because there's something I wanted to ask you. The thing is, I was—'

'Wait for me! Oh, no, my hair's going to go frizzy, I can feel it happening!'

'You wimp, don't moan! Anyway, the rain's stopped. Mind your shoes in that puddle!'

The two girls, one dark and one blonde, were glamorous and beautifully if somewhat inappropriately dressed. But the rain had indeed stopped as suddenly as it had begun. Clutching expensive-looking handbags and teetering on sky-high heels, they were each carrying cellophane-wrapped white roses. Mel's stomach disappeared as they reached Alex's grave and screeched to a halt.

'Here it is! Here's Alex. Oh look, someone else has left flowers too.'

Next to her, James murmured in Mel's ear, 'Who's that?'

Terrified she might actually be sick with nerves, Mel shook her head and croaked, 'Don't know.'

'Darling Alex, oh God, I miss you so much. Had to come and see you today,' said the blonde. 'It's my hen night – I'm getting married again! Can you believe it?'

The dark-haired one put her arm around her.

'Don't cry; you'll mess up your mascara.'

'I know, I know. I'm not going to.'

Fanning her face with long, scarlet-tipped fingers, the blonde watched as her friend unceremoniously tipped the dying chrysanthemums out of the vase and replaced them with the long-stemmed white roses.

Mel, watching them from twenty feet away, heard James's indignant intake of breath. Furious on her behalf he whispered in her ear, 'Who are they?'

'Just . . . just wait.'

It was all she could say at the moment. As soon as the girls were gone, she would explain. And they didn't appear to be intending to hang around.

'OK, taxi's waiting so we need to get off now.'

The blonde blew a kiss at the headstone. 'Love you so much though, yeah? Miss you loads. Hope you like the flowers.'

'Come on, then.' Linking arms, the brunette said, 'We've done our bit. Wonder who left those things though, eh?' She indicated the faded red and orange blooms now lying scattered on the ground.

'God only knows,' the blonde grimaced. 'Can't have

known Alex very well if they thought she'd like them. What was it she always said? Champagne, diamonds and perfect white roses every time!'

'Hey.' James caught up with her outside the cemetery.

'I'm sorry, so sorry. It's all in there.' Mel nodded at the letter she'd thrust into his hand before taking off. 'And I'm not really mad. I just did a mad thing.' Trembling with shame, she watched him read it.

'Why?'

'Because I thought you looked nice. And I thought – like an idiot – that it would be a way we could carry on bumping into each other.'

'I already knew that,' said James.

She stared back at him. 'What?'

'Well, I knew Alex was a girl. Her grandmother used to visit her grave and show me photos of her. So I kind of guessed that might be why you were doing it.' He smiled. 'Hoped so, anyway.'

'Are you serious?'

'Seems that way.'

The dimple was back.

'And if it helps, it's exactly the kind of mad thing Suzannah would have done in your situation. So . . . are you in a rush to get home, or do you fancy trying out that new restaurant on Hope Street?'

Mel blinked and attempted to slow her breathing. He actually seemed to mean it. At last she said, 'Well, I suppose we could give it a go.'

The Ministry of Whisky

BY VAL McDERMID

*T*here are two things everybody knows about John French the minister – he likes a dram, and his wife won't have a drop in the house. That's why he spends as much time as possible out and about, making himself at home with his parishioners. Even the strictest teetotallers, the dry alcoholics and the three English families understand they have to keep whisky in the house for the minister. Newcomers to the parish who don't know the drill get their first visit seasoned with a heavy-handed version of the Wedding at Cana, complete with knowing winks and exaggerated gestures. If they don't get the message, Mr French mentions in passing to one of the kirk elders that such-and-such a body doesn't seem to have much grasp of the rules of hospitality. Then the elder has a quiet word ahead of the minister's next pastoral visit. Trust me, most folks don't have to be told twice.

Don't get me wrong, Mr French is no drunk. I'm born and bred in Inverbiggin, and I've never seen him the worse for drink. I know who the village drunks are, and the minister isn't one of them. OK, he maybe spends his life a bit blurred round the edges, but you can hardly blame him for that. We all need something to help us deal with life's little disappointments. And God knows, the minister has that to do twenty-four-seven. Because I don't think for a minute that Inverbiggin is where he planned to end up.

I've seen folks' wedding photos with Mr French when he first came here. God, but he was handsome. You can still see it now, even though he's definitely past his best. Back then, though, he looked like a cross between Robert Redford and the kind of pop star your granny would approve of. A thick mane of reddish-blond hair, square jaw, broad shoulders and a gleaming row of teeth that were a lot closer to perfection than you generally saw in the backwoods of Stirlingshire back then. The looks have faded, inevitably, though he'd still give most of the men round here a run for their money. What's more important is that he's still a brilliant preacher. At least half his congregation are agnostic – if not downright atheist – but we all still turn up on a Sunday for the pure pleasure of listening to him. It's better than anything you get on the telly, because it's rooted in our community. So imagine what a catch he was back when he started out, when he was good-looking and he could preach. Obviously, his natural home would have been some showpiece congregation in Glasgow or Edinburgh. The man has ex-future Moderator of the Church of Scotland written all over him.

Something obviously went badly wrong for him to

end up here. Even its best friends would have to admit that Inverbiggin is one of the last stops on the road to nowhere. I don't know what it was that he did in the dim and distant past to blot his copybook, but it can't have been trivial for him to be sent this far into exile. Mind you, back when he arrived here thirty-odd years ago, the Church of Scotland was a lot closer to the Wee Frees than it is these days. So maybe all he did was have a hurl on the kids' swings in the park on a Sunday when they should have been chained up. Whatever. One way or another, he must have really pissed somebody off.

I don't know whether his wife knows the full story behind their exile, but she sure as hell knows she's been banished. There's no way this is her natural habitat either. She should be in some posh part of Glasgow or Edinburgh, hosting wee soirées to raise money for Darfur or Gaza. One time, and one time only, she unbent enough to speak to me at the summer fete when we got stuck together on the tombola. 'He's a good man,' she said, her eye on Mr French as he glad-handed his way round the stalls. She gave me a look sharp as Jessie Robertson's tongue. 'He deserves to be among good people.' Her meaning was clear. And I couldn't find it in my heart to disagree with her.

Her obvious bitterness is neutralised by the sweetness of her husband. Mr French might have had high-flying ambitions, but having his dreams trashed hasn't left him resentful or frustrated. It's pretty amazing, really, but in exchange for the whisky he's given us compassion and comprehension. Fuelled by a succession of drams, he seems to find a way to the heart of what we all need from him. It's not a one-way street either. The more he answers the challenge of meeting our needs, the finer the whisky that makes its way into his glass.

When he first started making his rounds, folk would pour any old rubbish. Crappy bargain blends that provoked instant indigestion, brutal supermarket own-brands that ripped the taste buds from your tongue, evil no-name rotgut provided by somebody's brother-in-law's best pal that made you think you were going blind. But gradually, his Good Samaritan acts spread through the community till there was hardly a household in Inverbiggin that hadn't been touched by them. Our way of saying thank you was to provide better drink. Quality blends, single malts, single-barrel vintages. You scratch my back, I'll scratch yours.

See, we all find our own ways to cope with living in Inverbiggin. The minister and his wife aren't the only ones who started out with higher hopes. Maybe it's precisely because his own dreams were dashed that he handles our failures so well. He intervenes when other people would be too scared or too discouraged to get in the middle of things. Kids that are slipping through the cracks at school – John French grabs the bull by the horns and takes on the teachers as well as the parents. Carers doing stuff for parents and disabled kids that none of us can think about without shuddering – John

French goes to bat for them and scores relief and respite.

And then there was that business with Kirsty Black. Everybody knew things were far from right between her and her man. But she'd made her bed, and we were all content to let her lie on it. At least if he was taking out his rage on her, William Black was leaving other folk alone.

I must have been about twelve years old when I discovered why William Black was known as BB, a man notorious for his willingness to pick a fight with anybody about anything. 'He thinks it stands for Big Bill,' my father told me after I'd had the misfortune to witness BB Black smash a man's face to pulp outside the chip shop. 'But everybody else in Inverbiggin knows it stands for Bad Bastard.' My father was no angel either, but his darkness was more devious. I got the feeling he despised BB as much for his lack of subtlety as for the violence itself.

When Kirsty lost her first baby in the fifth month of her pregnancy, we all knew by the next teatime that it had happened because BB Black had knocked her down and kicked her in the belly. We all knew because Betty McEwan, the midwife, heard it from one of the nurses at the infirmary who apparently said you could see the mark of his boot on her belly. But Kirsty was adamant that she'd fallen getting out of the bath. So that was that. No point in calling in the police or the social services if Kirsty couldn't manage to stick up for herself.

Wee towns like Inverbiggin are supposed to be all about community, all about looking out for each other. But we can turn a blind eye as surely as any block of flats in the big city. We all got extremely good at looking the other way when Kirsty walked by.

All except John French. He saw the bruises, he saw how Kirsty flinched when anybody spoke to her, he saw the awkward way she held herself when her ribs were bruised and cracked. He tried to persuade her to leave her man, but she was too scared. She had no place to go and by then, she had two kids. The minister suggested a refuge, but Kirsty was almost as afraid of being cast adrift among strangers as she was of William Black himself. So then Mr French said he would talk to the Bad Bastard, to put him on notice that somebody was on to him. But Kirsty pleaded with the minister to stay out of it, and he eventually gave in to her wishes.

I know all this because it came out at the trial. Kirsty wasn't able to give evidence herself. She was catatonic by that point. But Mr French stood in the witness box and explained to the court that Kirsty had exhibited all the signs of a woman who had been reduced to a zombie-like state by violence and terror. He told them she had been determined to protect her kids. That she'd been in fear for her own life and the lives of her children that Friday night when he'd come home roaring drunk, and she'd picked up the kitchen knife and thrust it up into William Black's soft belly.

You could see the jury loved John French. They'd

have taken him home and sat him on the mantelpiece just for the sheer pleasure of listening to him and looking at him. He surfed the courtroom like a man riding on the crest of a wave of righteousness rather than a wave of whisky.

The prosecution didn't stand a chance. The jury went for the 'not proven' verdict on the culpable homicide charge, and Kirsty walked out of the court a free woman. It took some more work from Mr French, but eventually her lawyers got the kids back from social services and she moved back home. Everybody rallied round. I suppose ignoring what had happened to Kirsty kind of guilt-tripped us all into lending a helping hand. Better late than never, the minister pointed out one Sunday when he gave us his particular take on the Good Samaritan story. He was adamant that we should open our hearts and put our faith in God.

But here's the thing about people like John French. Like his wife said, he does deserve to be among good people. Because being ready to think the best of folk leaves you wide open to the ones that can't wait to take advantage. And there are one or two like that in Inver-biggin.

Take me, for example. I've been out of love with my husband for years. He's a coarse, uncouth, ignorant pig. He's never dared to lift a hand to me, but he disgusts me. Worse still, he bores the living daylights out of me. When he walks in a room, he sucks the life out of it. There is one positive thing about my husband, though. His job comes with terrific death-in-service benefits.

And then there's that lovely big insurance policy. Frankly, it'll be worth every penny I've spent on rare malts and exclusive single-barrel vintages.

Because I've been planting the seeds for a while now. I used to do amateur dramatics years ago. I can play my part well, and I can paint a bonny set of bruises on my back and my ribs. Good enough to fool a man whose vocation would never let him examine a woman's injuries too closely. I even got him to take some photos on my mobile phone. If the police examine them later, they won't be able to make out too much detail, which suits me just fine. And after all, there's precedent now. Nobody would dare to doubt John French, not after the publicity Kirsty's case earned him.

Never mind putting my faith in God. Me, I'm putting my faith in John French and the ministry of whisky.

The Spirit of Summer

BY KATE MOSSE

*I*magine a photograph in an album, the corners frayed and brittle. A keepsake of a moment. The drowsy hollow of an afternoon in August, of a holiday in France, where the air hangs still and shimmering. You see yourself, bare arms and hair twisted up in a grip, beaded sandals and a favourite dress. A straw hat on the bench beside you and a paperback book open in your lap.

Look at the snapshot and remember. Pretend it's you in the photograph. There you are, see? Sitting on one of those benches, the metal imprinting its pattern on the backs of your legs. An ordinary bench, in an ordinary park, on an ordinary day in August.

At first, you don't see the woman. Or rather, you see her, but you don't pay much attention. Your eyes slip, impersonally, over her, though you do notice how pale she is. White almost, blue almost, translucent skin in the sleeping afternoon. And you look down at your own arms, tanned by the Languedocien sun, and you are pleased.

The heat was unforgiving, remember? Pinching at

your cheeks and your arms as you watch your daughter – a small six-year-old, but tough, a *garçon manqué*, as the French put it – scramble up and along the climbing frame. And you think to yourself that you must not worry. If she were to fall – which she won't, she won't – then at least there's sand beneath the monkey bars. That you mustn't fuss, mustn't interfere or spoil.

What else? Look at the photograph in the album once more and recognise that familiar, that distant look. The memory of grief and of loss, those eyes haunted by the echo of deep emotion felt and accepted some years ago. Without the support of your friends, the consoling company of women, you would have gone under.

You keep saying this to yourself, though you know it is not entirely true. Being a mother keeps you bound to the earth. No parent abandons her child because she is suffering or because she is lonely. Besides, such violent grief is in the past – Naomi only hours old, unaware of a car skidding in the rain in the car park of the maternity unit, metal connecting with skin and bone. He didn't know what hit him, they said. A freak accident, they said. Unlucky. A slick of oil and blood on the damp tarmac.

The pain is a dull ache now. And in these past six years, you've done all the right things and in the right order – the denial, then the anger and bargaining, the depression and, finally, acceptance. The status quo is captured, here, in this photograph. This woman – you – alone in Carcassonne watching Naomi play. She has found a friend, out of sight of the camera. The lack of a common language is no barrier to imagination. The desire to communicate is stronger than words – pointing, miming, tracing patterns in the dust with toes and sandals and twigs.

Drop your eyes to the novel you're pretending to read, the same page for the past half an hour. It's a beguiling story by a Chinese-American writer about August, the month of hungry ghosts, but the book's there for company rather than entertainment, and its words don't hold you.

So yes, the photograph tells the truth. It records the ordinary August afternoon as it happened. It is over now.

The truth? Well yes, but only so far as it goes. Your eyes drift to the silhouettes of the cypress trees of the Cimetière de Saint-Vincent on the hill overlooking Carcassonne. From behind the wall, just visible, the tip of a cross and stone angels and the roof of a sepulchre. And as you look up, beyond the voices of the children and the murmurings of the *gran'mères* and the occasional blast of a car horn, you feel the seductive tug of silence. You wish, just for a moment at least, that you could let go and join the silent sleepers in that quiet earth.

'*S'il vous plaît?*'

Your head shoots round to see the woman is standing in front of you. You experience a spurt of irritation that she should wish to sit beside you on this particular bench, when there are plenty of other free seats. But your desire for the grave makes you guilty, as if the thought is forerunner to the deed, and in any case you are polite by nature. So you smile and you gesture that she might join you.

'Of course,' you say, then repeat yourself in French.

The woman has no companionable book, no shopping basket nor, so far as you could tell, child in the park. But such very pale skin, so very transparent in the green shade beneath the *platanes*. The woman's hair is rolled off her face, and she's wearing a short-sleeved white dress with large buttons, cinched tight at the waist; there's something old-fashioned about it. Court shoes with a strap, tiny heels. Your eyes drop down once more to the pages of your paperback, but the characters are strangers. You can't remember why they are setting an extra place at the table or for whom.

And beyond the sounds of the playground, all sounds seem muffled now. The percussive tap and clink of barges on the Canal du Midi, or the groan of the lock gates or the shriek of a train drawing into the railway station, all audible still but at the same time, distant. For a moment, silence suspended, then the chimes of the bells of Saint-Vincent striking the quarter-hour, answered by the bells of the Cathédrale Saint-Michel an instant later.

'It is a relief, don't you find, the peace.'

Her voice was lower than you might have expected, deeper, with an echo of some other hidden story. Remember?

'I suppose so,' you say.

'All the same, you wish to leave?'

You are offended at this presumption of intimacy, though you're not sure why. You glance at Naomi, at home in her imaginary world with her new friend.

'Not at all,' you say. 'My daughter . . .'

The woman is nodding, as if the words are some kind of confession.

'Yes, there's the pity of it.'

'No,' you say, more sharply than you intend. 'What I mean is, I'm happy to wait until she's ready.'

'Je sais.'

You frown. What does the woman mean, saying she knows? Knows what? The words echo in your head and, as they do, you are aware of her expression altering as if she is hearing something, perceiving something private, that should remain hidden. You are looking around the playground now, hoping for some polite escape, but all the benches are now, suddenly, occupied.

Because you do not wish either to be rude or to spoil your daughter's afternoon, you are obliged to stay put. Then she speaks again. This time, it is an ordinary question, and you are reassured.

'You are on holiday?'

'Yes,' you say. 'A little sightseeing, the beach at Narbonne, the usual sort of thing.'

'Pleasant.'

'Yes.' You pause. 'You're from around here?'

She looks at you now, grey eyes, clear. 'I lived most of my life on the Quai Riquet, down under the bridge there on the Route de Minervois.'

You follow the woman's trailing arm pointing towards the Canal du Midi, then you nod.

'But you don't live in Carcassonne any more?'

She sighs, a sound that seems to carry within it weariness and fatigue, but also sympathy. Hope.

'You have the choice to go, should you wish. To stay, should you wish.'

You shake your head at the misunderstanding – it is your daughter's wishes, not your own, that dictate the pattern of your life – but you smile anyway.

'I know,' you say. Then, for a reason you do not quite understand, you add: 'Thank you.'

She reflects your own smile back at you. '*Je vous en prie*. It is my pleasure.'

Was it then you held out your hand? Light, cold, the slightest of touches, the photograph tells you nothing of what came before or after. Was it then that you gave her your name and she gave you hers, or did that happen earlier?

'Marie,' she says. 'Marie Fournes.'

But, at that moment, your daughter comes over with her new friend, smiling and laughing and asking if they might have an ice cream. The French child has a Polaroid camera and lets Naomi take a snap, and you pull a silly face for the girls. You rest the photograph, grey and sticky, on the paperback novel while the image develops and you open your purse and find a couple of francs, one for each little girl's hand, and say you'll take a photograph of them with their ices when they come back. And by the time all this has happened

– seconds, minutes, who's to say – you turn back to Marie to apologise for the interruption, and you find she is no longer there.

You look around – the playground, towards the street, up towards the men playing boules, behind at the lapping water of the Canal du Midi – but she's nowhere to be seen. You slump back on the bench, surprised and disappointed that she has gone without saying goodbye.

You look down at the image on your lap, at your own outline developing in front of your eyes, thinking perhaps to see her sitting beside you. The angle is wrong, though, and it's only you there, alone on the bench. Or is there an echo beside you, like the shadow of Branwell Brontë in the painting with his sisters? You peer harder, but before you have a moment to think, your daughter has tumbled back with the change and a blue Mr Freeze.

'The lady who was here with me, darling,' you say. 'Did you see where she went?'

Naomi shrugs, impatient to be back to her *copine*, then pauses. Still, for a moment. She points at the photograph in your lap.

'You look different,' she says.

'I do?'

'Yes,' she nods in an exaggerated way, part mime, part confirmation. 'You're smiling.'

Then she's off again, running back to the climbing frame and the sand and her imaginary world.

You look down and see it's true. You do look

different. At peace, perhaps. Content, perhaps. Your eyes, once more, glance around the playground, seeing the same things as before, yet this time seeing life, seeing possibilities, as if the colour is coming back to the world. And when you look up to the Cimetière de Saint-Vincent on the hill, you feel nothing but pleasure at the beauty of the old grey stone and the enduring architecture and statues.

The shadows begin to dip. The air begins to cool. It's the time when, usually, you leave the playground and return to your campsite below the medieval *cité* on the far side of the river.

Along the Canal du Midi, beneath the bridge on the Quai Riquet – at the place where twenty people were murdered on 20 August 1944 in the dying days of the War – for an instant, the setting sun strikes the brass plaque and illuminates one name in particular: *Fournes Marie*.

The shadows stretch further, slatted beams of late-afternoon light falling between the trees, the sounds of early evening. Ice in a glass, the pop of a wine cork, fragments of music filtering out from the bar of the Brasserie Terminus on the opposite corner.

'Can we stay a little longer?' Naomi asks. 'Please, just five more minutes? Please?'

And now you understand. And you look down at the photograph in your lap, at your daughter's eager face, at the space on the bench where the woman sat.

'Of course,' you say. 'We can stay as long as we like.'

Last Year's Coat

BY JOJO MOYES

*T*he lining of the coat has gone completely. Evie holds it up and runs her finger along the ripped seam, wondering if there is any way she can pull the fine edges of frayed fabric together. She turns it over, looking at the thinned wool, the slight sheen on the elbows, and realises there is little point.

She knows exactly what she would buy in its place. She sees it in the window of the shop twice a day as she walks past, slowing her stride a little just to gaze at it. Midnight blue, with a silvery lambswool collar; classic enough to last several years, but just different enough not to look like every other chain-store coat.

It costs £185.

Evie puts her head down and walks past.

Not that long ago, Evie would have bought the coat. She would have held it up in her lunch hour, modelled it in front of the girls in Marketing, carried it home in its expensive bag, its weight banging satisfyingly against her legs.

But some time ago, without apparently applying, they seem to have become official members of the

Squeezed Middle. Pete's hours were abruptly cut by thirty per cent. The weekly grocery bill went up by fifteen per cent. Fuel is so expensive that they sold her car and she now walks the two miles to work. Heating, a luxury, comes on for an hour in the morning and two at night. The mortgage that had seemed so manageable now hangs over them like a great albatross. She sits at the kitchen table in the evenings, poring over columns of figures, warning her teenage daughters against unnecessary expenditure like her own mother had warned her about Bad Men.

'C'mon, love. Let's go to bed.' Pete's hands land gently on her shoulders.

'I'm doing the accounts.'

'Then let's go and huddle together for bodily warmth. I'm only thinking of our heating bill,' he adds, solemnly. 'Honest. I won't enjoy it at all.'

Her smile is weak, a reflexive thing. He puts his arms around her. 'Come on, lovely. We'll be fine. We've got through worse.'

She knows he is right. At least they are both in work. They have friends who paint on brittle smiles, bat away enquiries about new jobs with a vague, 'Oh . . . got a few things in the pipeline.' Two have sold their houses and downsized, citing 'family reasons'.

'How's your dad?'

'Not bad.' Every evening Pete goes over after work, taking him a hot meal. 'The car's not right, though.'

'Don't say that!'

'I know. I think the starter motor is going. Look, don't panic. I'll pop it into Mike's, see if he can give us a good price.'

She does not mention the coat.

The girls in Marketing do not fret about starter motors or heating bills. They still disappear at lunchtimes, returning to show off their purchases with the beady-eyed acquisitiveness of a hunter returning with a skin. They arrive on Monday mornings bearing tales of city breaks in Paris and Lisbon, eat out weekly at the pizza restaurant (Evie insists that, really, she's quite happy with her cheese sandwiches). She tries not to feel resentful. Two of them don't have children; Felicity has a husband who earns three times what she does. I have Pete and the girls, she tells herself firmly, and we are all healthy and we have a roof over our heads. But sometimes when she hears them talking about Barcelona, or showing off yet another pair of shoes, her jaw clenches so hard she fears for her tooth enamel.

'I need a new coat,' she tells Pete finally. She says it like someone admitting an infidelity.

'You've got loads of coats, surely.'

'Nope. I've had this four years, my mackintosh and that black one I got off eBay, where the sleeve fell apart.'

Pete shrugs. 'So? You need a coat, go buy a coat.'

'But the only one I like is expensive.'

'How expensive?'

She tells him and watches him blanch. Pete thinks

that spending more than six quid on a haircut is a sign of insanity. The downside of her running the family's accounts is that his cost thermostat is still set somewhere in the mid-eighties.

'Is that a . . . designer coat?'

'No. Just a good wool coat.'

He is silent. 'There's Kate's school trip. And my starter motor.'

'I know. It's OK. I'm not going to buy it.'

The next morning she crosses the road when she walks to work, just so she cannot see it. But the coat has lodged itself firmly in her mind's eye. She sees it every time she catches her fingers in her ripped lining. She sees it when Felicity returns from lunch with a new coat (red, silk lining) of her own. It feels somehow symbolic of everything that has gone wrong with their lives.

'We'll get you a coat,' says Pete on Saturday. 'I'm sure we can find one you like.'

They stop in front of the shop window and she looks at him mutely. He squeezes her arm. They walk on through several more shops and finally to Get the Look, a store her daughters like; it is full of 'fun' fashion, and the music is deafening. Pete normally hates shopping, but seems to realise how down she is. He rifles through the rails, holds up a dark blue coat with a fake-fur collar. 'Look – it's like that one you like! And it's only . . .' he peers at the label, 'twenty-nine pounds!'

She allows him to slide it on her and she looks at herself in the mirror.

The coat is slightly too tight under the arms. The collar is nice, but she suspects it will look matted within weeks. The cut seems to stretch and sag in just the wrong places. The wool mix is mostly synthetic.

'You look gorgeous,' Pete says.

Pete would say she looked gorgeous if she was wearing prison scrubs. She hates this coat. She knows that every time she puts it on it will feel like a silent rebuke. Forty-three years old, and you are wearing a cheap coat from the teenagers' shop.

'I'll think about it,' she says.

Lunchtimes have become a kind of torture. Today the girls in Marketing are booking tickets; a resurrected boy band last popular fifteen years ago.

'Fancy it, Evie? Girls' night out?'

She looks at the ticket prices: seventy-five quid, plus transport.

'Not me,' she smiles. 'I never much liked them the first time round.'

It is a lie, of course. She adored them. She stomps home, allowing the coat only the briefest glance. She feels childish, mutinous. And then she sees Pete's legs sticking out from under the car.

'What are you doing out here? It's raining.'

'I thought I'd have a go at the car myself. Save a few bob.'

'But you know nothing about cars.'

'I downloaded some stuff off the Internet. And Mike said he'd take a look afterwards, to check I've done everything right.'

She gazes at him. He always had been resourceful.

'Have you been to your dad's?'

'Yeah. I got the bus.'

Evie stares at her husband's soaked, blackened trousers and sighs. 'I'll make him a casserole so that if you can't make it there for a couple of days, he'll still have something to eat.'

'You're a star.' He blows her a kiss with oily fingers.

Perhaps picking up on her subdued mood, the girls are sweet over supper. Pete is preoccupied, gazing at printed diagrams of engine innards. Evie tells herself there are worse things than not being able to afford the coat you really want.

'I'll get that twenty-nine-pound coat tomorrow. If it's all right with you.'

'You looked lovely in it.' Pete kisses her head. She can see from his face that he knows how much she hates it. When the girls leave the table, he says softly, 'Things will change, you know.'

Felicity has a new handbag. Evie tries to ignore the distant commotion as it is pulled from its box, birthed from its cotton cover and held up for the others to admire; the kind of bag that costs a month's salary. Evie pretends to be absorbed by spreadsheets so that she doesn't have to look. She is embarrassed by the waves of envy that steal over her as she hears the oohs and aahs of admiration.

But it does not stop there. Myra has ordered a new sofa. The girls discuss their forthcoming night out. Felicity sits her bag on top of her desk and makes jokes about loving it more than a baby.

Evie heads for Get the Look at lunchtime. She walks blindly, her head dipped, telling herself it's just a coat. And then she stops outside the other boutique, halted by the big red sign in the window. SALE. Her heart gives a lurch.

She is inside, her heart beating, refusing to listen to the little voice in her head.

'The blue wool coat,' she says to the assistant. 'How much is it reduced by?'

'Everything in the window is half price, madam.'

Ninety pounds. Yes, it's still expensive, but it's half price. Surely that counts for something? 'I'll have the size twelve,' she says, before reason can seep in.

The assistant returns from the rails as Evie is pulling her credit card from her bag. It's a beautiful coat, she tells herself. It will last for years. Pete will understand.

'I'm so sorry, madam. The size twelve has gone. And that was our last one.'

'What?'

'So sorry.'

Evie is deflated. She gazes over at the window and slides her purse back into her bag. She raises a small, defeated smile. 'Never mind. It's probably just as well.' She does not go on to Get the Look. Right now, she would rather stick with last year's coat.

*

'Hey you.'

She is hanging up her coat when Pete puts his head around the door. She closes her eyes as he kisses her.

'You're wet.'

'It's raining.'

'You should have told me. I'd have come and picked you up.'

'Is the car working?'

'For now. Mike said I actually did a good job. How amazing am I?'

'Amazing.'

She holds him for a minute, then walks through to the comforting fug of her kitchen. One of the girls has been making cookies, and she inhales the leftover scent of baking.

'Oh. And there's something for you on the table.'

Evie glances over and sees the bag. She stares at Pete.

'What's this?'

'Open it.'

She lifts the side of the bag and peers inside. She freezes.

'Don't panic. It's from Dad. For all the meals.'

'What?'

'He says he can't keep accepting your food unless you let him give something back. You know what he's like. I told him about the coat, and you wouldn't believe it – there was only a bloody sale on. We picked it up at lunchtime.'

'Your dad bought me a coat?'

'Don't get all tearful. He reckoned it was the equivalent of thirty steak pies and twenty of your crumbles. He says it's actually pretty good value.'

Evie walks to work. She is early; the office is almost empty. Felicity disappears to the Ladies to do her make-up, and Evie hums as she drops the marketing budgets on her desk. As she passes, she sees a statement sticking out from under the designer bag and steps back, checking if it is a company account. But it's personal; a credit-card statement. Evie glimpses the total and blinks.

But it really is five figures.

'Are you coming out?' says Felicity at lunchtime. 'We thought we'd try the new Thai place. Show off your new coat!'

Evie thinks for a minute, then pulls her lunch from her bag. 'Not today,' she says. 'But thanks anyway.'

As they leave, she turns and carefully straightens her coat on the back of her chair, smoothing the collar. And even though she is not massively fond of cheese sandwiches, Evie smiles.

The Invitation

BY ADELE PARKS

*H*elen's transfer from the Liverpool office to the smaller office in Chester had come along at exactly the right time, and she knew she had to maximise the opportunity. So she'd promised herself that she'd accept every invite that fluttered her way. So far, this meant she'd had to dig out flat shoes and amble around Westminster Park (commenting on the impressive landscaping), go to the Monday quiz night at The Crown (to answer questions on sport and politics), and get up early on a Sunday morning to play badminton (even though she hadn't held a racket since she was in sixth form, over twenty years ago). She had not allowed for shyness, or even personal taste.

In Liverpool Helen had been stuck in a rut – emotionally and professionally – for far too long. Liverpool was rammed with haunting memories of her ex, Peter, even though they'd divorced three years ago. She had occasionally dated since then, because everybody – from her mother to her best friend to her teenage nieces – said she ought to, but her broken heart wasn't in it and the men she dated soon became aware of this. A clean start was exactly what was required; she needed to know that she could confidently walk around Waitrose without dreading bumping into Peter and his new wife; she wanted to be able to go to a bar or restaurant without being bludgeoned with memories of times she'd visited the same place as half a happy couple.

The only problem was, despite the undoubted efficiency of the company's relocations manager, a clean start required a lot of effort. The relocations manager had shown Helen four equally lovely one-bed apartments; she settled on the one nearest the park because Helen was thinking about getting a dog, or a bike, or something that would indicate that she had a life. The relocations manager registered her at a doctor's and dentist's surgery. She even left a list of decent hair salons. The difficulty was making new friends. Helen realised that she had to make some, but she secretly felt a little bit old for making new friends. It's easy when you're eight; you simply share a Curly Wurly or offer to turn the skipping rope. Not so easy at thirty-eight. The relocations manager couldn't help her with that one.

At work, a woman called Louise swept Helen under her wing. Helen gratefully snuggled there because they were the same grade middle management, the same age and when they selected their lunches in the canteen, it transpired that they had the same taste in yogurts; Helen hoped it was enough to kick-start a friendship. The notable differences between them were that Louise was married with two sons and she lived in a large town house. She was so proud of her husband, boys and town house that she threw elaborate dinner parties every Saturday so that she could share her good fortune, and no doubt showcase it too, Helen thought, as she tried not to feel aggrieved by the glaring disparity. Louise invited Helen for dinner.

All week, Louise excitedly chattered about the menu and guests. She was planning on serving monkfish and scallops with wood-roasted vegetables. Helen knew that Louise would also be serving up an eligible man for Helen's delectation. Helen knew the dinner-party formula: three couples, her and a spare man. The marrieds looked to the singletons for entertainment. Would they or wouldn't they share a taxi home? Her married pals back in Liverpool had done exactly the same thing: potential boyfriends were recruited with Kitchener enthusiasm. Helen knew that intentions were good. A happily married woman like Louise was simply unable to resist matchmaking, however Helen dreaded the evening.

It turned out to be exactly as expected; the food was marvellous, the guests were pleasant but not profound and the spare man was disinterested, possibly even gay. Conversation centred around children's schools and the difficulty in securing a trustworthy builder. They drank moderately because no one wanted hangovers any more – they couldn't afford to lose their Sunday mornings to such messiness. Helen went through the motions – these concerns weren't hers, but she was sympathetic and familiar enough with them to make the appropriate comments in the correct places. The only surprise was Louise's husband, Ned.

Helen had been expecting a middle-aged guy fighting his paunch and the weight of his mortgage. But in fact Louise's husband was quite exceptionally striking; classically tall, dark and handsome, with cheekbones you could cut yourself on. Helen would never, ever look at a man that was taken – she'd been on the wrong end of infidelity – however, she couldn't fail to be impressed.

Until she talked to him. Ned was a bit dull for her taste. He was perfectly pleasant, not rude or aggressive or overwhelmingly cocksure (frankly any of those alternatives might have been more exciting) – he was simply boring. He spoke for fifteen uninterrupted minutes about the best garden weedkiller available on the market. Louise beamed throughout his monologue, seemingly unaware that her guests had nodded off. When they said goodnight, Louise pulled Helen into a hug and whispered, 'I know that one day you'll find someone just as wonderfully dependable as my Ned.' Helen appreciated the sentiment and therefore bit her tongue, resisting commenting that she'd prefer to stay single than suffer a slow death by tedium, even if her killer was so utterly handsome. Each to their own, she thought as she got into the back of the cab.

The next invite Helen received was from Sharon in Accounts, who asked her to join a gang of colleagues for a drink in town. When Louise heard that Helen was going to Hoopers Bar, she had looked concerned.

'It's a cattle market. That bar attracts the wrong sort.'

'Which sort, exactly?'

'People just out for a good time, if you know what I mean.'

Helen thought that people just out for a good time would be a welcome break from people who had forgotten how to have a good time, and so promptly accepted Sharon's invite.

As Helen pushed open the door to the packed wine bar she was hit by the smell of bodies and booze, by the loud music and the equally loud shirts. Everyone there was clearly jacked up on irresponsibility, a powerful aphrodisiac. Helen hadn't been to this kind of bar, full of intensely alluring types, for ages. It was in a bar like this that she'd met Peter, a lifetime ago. She was just thinking that she might very well enjoy herself, if not for the novelty factor alone, when she saw him. He was sat at the bar, surrounded by a bevy of young blondes, clearly having the time of his life. Ned.

Helen didn't stay long after that. Just long enough to see Ned slide his arm around the most attractive girl's waist. Her blood slowed. Poor Louise; poor trusting, content, loving Louise. After Peter had left Helen and the storm of tears and regrets had finally subsided, two of her friends came forward and said they'd long since suspected him of having an affair. One said she'd actually seen him with the other woman. Helen had felt betrayed all over again. Why hadn't they told her? Warned her? Prepared her? Her friends had muttered something about messengers being shot. She hadn't understood at the time, but now she did. She didn't want to be the one to bring the bad news to Louise's door.

The following week, Helen arranged to go for dinner with a gang from Marketing. The guy who issued the invite said that she'd 'make up the numbers'. He said this in an offhand way that made her doubt the evening would be the first step on the path to true love, but she accepted anyway because every invite had to be honoured. As she scampered into the restaurant and out of the rain, she literally bumped into him. Ned. This time he was with a brunette, who was throwing back her head and screaming with laughter. Helen couldn't imagine what Ned might have said that was so funny.

'Sorry,' he murmured to Helen as she wobbled with the force of their collision. 'You OK?' Then he flashed the most charming smile, and it didn't falter even when he stared right at her. In fact, in the moment he must have registered who he'd bumped into, Ned's smile broadened a fraction further. The rat. Helen was struck dumb by his audacity, and she watched helplessly as he hailed a taxi and drove away with his brunette.

Naturally, the evening was unsuccessful. Helen was in turmoil. Louise's husband was not having an affair, he was a serial philanderer! Poor Louise, those poor boys. What could Helen do? After lengthy consideration she decided that when she next spotted Ned, she'd tackle him. Make him see that his careless womanising was unacceptable. That it was in fact a declaration of war.

Helen didn't have to wait long. The following

Thursday she agreed to go for a drink with a group of women from her bums-and-tums class. They selected a quiet wine bar where it was possible to hold a conversation; mellow lounge music floated past the enormous potted plants, and there was a menu of wines to savour. Helen thought it was a great find – until she spotted him.

This time, he was with a stunning redhead. It was heinous to admit that they made a striking couple, yet brilliant to note that the date was clearly going badly; Ned kept looking at his watch and the redhead seemed more interested in the menu than him. Helen slunk behind a potted plant and bided her time. After just fifteen minutes the redhead stood up, coolly kissed Ned on the cheek and said her goodbyes. Helen felt a jolt of delight and relief that tonight, at least, Ned hadn't got lucky. Would he now scuttle home to Louise? It wasn't a comforting thought, but what was the solution? As Ned waved for the bill, Helen grabbed her courage and the moment.

She stood in front of him, hands on hips, and demanded, 'How could you?'

'Sorry?' Ned had the nerve to look unperturbed.

'What do you think you are playing at? In a small town such as this, you were bound to be spotted sooner rather than later. Not that you seem to be making much of an attempt at discretion.'

'I really think that—'

Helen cut him off. She'd heard all the excuses and clichés when she and Peter were splitting up, and she didn't want to hear them again. She wasn't going to allow another woman to suffer in the same way she had. So Ned was amazingly good-looking, and considering how he'd chatted to the blondes in Hoopers and the brunette outside the restaurant, quite clearly gifted with some sort of charm (although she hadn't been enthralled at his dinner party); well, good looks and charm shouldn't automatically lead to infidelity. It was vile. Ned didn't even have the decency to look ashamed. He looked unconcerned, although mildly confused by Helen's outburst.

'It's the blatancy, the cruel indifference to Louise that I find most shocking.'

'Oh, you are a friend of Louise's.' Ned's face cleared.

'Ned, we met at your house. Am I that forgettable?' she demanded angrily.

'You're very memorable. And now I see you are also loyal, feisty and beautiful.' Helen was incensed. Ned was hitting on her too, now! How dare he? 'But I'm not Ned. I'm Ben, Ned's twin brother. Single brother,' he added with a delicious slow smile that thumped Helen in the stomach.

'Oh. I thought . . .' Helen faltered, embarrassed, delighted and excited all at once.

Ben's smile broadened a fraction further. 'Yes, I can imagine what you thought. Now, I wonder, would you like a drink?'

Helen accepted. After all, she had promised herself that she'd accept every invite that came her way. It would be wrong not to.

Wabi-sabi

BY NICKY PELLEGRINO

or ages I've been a winter person. I like long boots and lots of layers, lovely chunky-knit scarves. Summer doesn't suit me, though it must have done once. I remember years of bare legs and flimsy fabrics; yes, even a striped blue bikini. But that was back when I woke up every morning to a flat stomach and smooth thighs. Nowadays, I prefer to cover the bits that wobble and dimple. Most women my age have them, don't they? Well, I like to keep mine hidden. So when Shelley said, 'Italy in August' and 'Divine villa near the coast' and 'Why don't you come, Kath? You could use a break', I wasn't tempted at all. I gave her a whole smorgasbord of excuses: 'Busy time at work' and 'Credit cards maxed out' and 'Bloody hot in August, isn't it?'

Shelley never has been one to take no for an answer. She forwarded me a link to the villa, and I had to admit it did look stunning. It was built from honey-coloured stone and surrounded by cypress trees; it even had a tower, for goodness' sake.

'We need one more person to make up the

numbers,' Shelley emailed. 'Come on, Kath, you'll love it. Nothing to do but relax, eat yummy food, read books.'

It had been a long day at work, and I was slumped on the sofa, my laptop on my knee, idly googling. I had no intention of going anywhere, but still found myself checking a few websites about the area. There was a food tour in the nearest town, and a church with some interesting thirteenth-century frescoes. There were picturesque walks and panoramic views. There was a market with local crafts, and a restaurant famous for doing amazing things with truffles.

Perhaps it was the thought of waking up to another day just like all the rest. Maybe it was the truffles. Pouring another glass of wine, I emailed Shelley back. 'How much?'

The rental deal was amazing, and it turned out flights from Stansted were really cheap too. I looked back through the photographs of the villa. It was gorgeous. 'OK,' I conceded. 'Count me in.'

I packed cleverly for that holiday. Wide-brimmed hats and loose, long-sleeved kaftans; lots of sarongs and linen pants; and one old swimming costume chucked in at the last minute, just in case.

On the flight over, I heard all about the villa. It was a palazzo, really, and the owner was a local winemaker who told Shelley this was the first time the place had been rented out.

It was dark when we arrived. The minivan trip from the airport had been long, steep and twisty, so all of us were tired. We found some wine glasses, toasted the holiday with a bottle of cheap bubbly then headed to our rooms, planning to explore properly in the morning.

I fell on to the cool sheets gratefully. With the shutters closed, the room was dark and I slept better and far later than usual.

When I opened my eyes, the first thing I noticed was the ceiling. It was crazed with cracks and sagged alarmingly. Next, I realised the floor seemed to be sloping. A damp and musty smell hung in the air; everything looked old and worn.

Throwing open the shutters, I took a proper look around. Paint was peeling from scarred walls, woodwork soft to the touch. The plumbing complained with a series of creaks when I turned on a tap, and the water was faintly brownish.

I went down to the kitchen, observing more signs of neglect on the way – spotted mirrors, a splintering handrail on the stairs, broken tiles on the hallway floor.

'Hello,' I called, pushing open the heavy wooden door. The kitchen smelled of coffee but no one was there.

They had left me a note next to a box of pastries. *Gone to the beach. Decided to let you sleep. Come and join us when you've had breakfast.*

I made myself a double espresso, took a custard-filled pastry and wandered out to the terrace. There I found a rusty wrought-iron table, a tangled garden of herbs and a rather remarkable view. Standing beside an old rock wall, looking through the olive trees and right across the vineyard, I sipped my coffee, reflecting on the now obvious reasons for the rental being such a bargain.

'Buongiorno, signora.' The voice was so hearty and near, I gave a little squeak of fright.

'Oh, my apologies, you were relaxing and I have startled you.'

'Yes, I . . . I'm sorry, who are you?'

'Excuse me. I am Francesco, your host. I have come to make sure you all arrived safely, that the place is to your satisfaction and everyone is happy.'

I stared at him. He was a heavyset man, round in the belly and perhaps a little jowly but still very handsome, with a thick head of greying hair, almond eyes and skin the sun had turned caramel.

'Is everything to your satisfaction?' he prompted.

'Well, the thing is . . .'

I looked back at the house. Ivy climbed over old stone glowing gold in the morning sun. A muslin curtain billowed from an open window. Suddenly I could smell jasmine.

'It's rather run-down, isn't it?'

Seeming surprised, he turned his eyes to the old palazzo.

Francesco looked back at me. He smiled. Holding out his hands, palms upwards, he said with a shrug, 'Wabi-sabi.'

'I'm sorry . . . what?'

'Wabi-sabi,' he repeated, smiling again, then turned and walked away.

The heat of the day was building but still I wasn't drawn to join the others at the beach. Instead I went to find my guidebook and my list of possible activities. It might be the perfect day for an ancient crypt, or a wall of frescoes; lunch at an outdoor café if I could find a shady spot; then an afternoon of shopping.

I'm a person who likes my own company, so I spent a pleasant few hours exploring Marina Della Roccia. I admired the medieval architecture, toured a marble works and found a food market where I bought a lump of Parmesan and some fresh peaches. In the afternoon the shopkeepers hung CLOSED signs on their doors and so, once I'd eaten lunch, there was nothing to do but return to the villa.

I was struck again by how shabby the place was. If the palazzo had been in Francesco's family for generations, I could only assume he didn't number any handymen among his ancestors. He had managed a few pleasant touches – urns of red geraniums were dotted along a wall, coloured lanterns had been strung in the branches of a tree above the wrought-iron dining table. But if you looked closely, it was apparent the whole place was crumbling.

'Wabi-sabi', Francesco had said, but I hadn't a clue what it meant. Perhaps it was an apology.

Someone had left two dusty bottles of red wine on the kitchen table. Their label showed an old woodcut illustration of the palazzo beneath the words *Castello*

Della Roccia. I was at least two glasses into the first bottle by the time the others appeared, all salty, sandy limbs and damp hair.

'The beach is fun, the sea's so lovely, you should have come,' they chorused.

That evening, we cooked lamb with rosemary on the wood-fired barbecue and ate dinner outside by the light of candles and lanterns. Shadowed by night, the palazzo looked softer and very nearly perfect.

In the next few days, I ticked off almost everything on my holiday 'to do' list. The food tour was fun and the walks worthwhile. The only thing left was to see the church frescoes in the town's main piazza. If nothing else, it would be cool inside a church.

To my mind, those frescoes were long overdue for restoration. The colours had lost their lustre, and one or two seemed smudged. I didn't stay in the church for long. Coming back outside, blinking in the light, I heard a hearty greeting.

'Buongiorno, signora!'

'Oh, Francesco, it's you, hello.'

'You've been to see our beautiful frescoes,' he remarked. 'They are in the style of Giotto – some say they may even have been painted by the artist himself.'

'In that case, you'd think they might have taken better care of them,' I remarked.

He looked surprised, then shrugged.

'Wabi-sabi,' he said, and made to turn away.

'Wait, Francesco. What does that mean? Wabi-sabi?'

'You've never heard of it?'

I shook my head.

'Truly? Come, let me buy you a drink and I'll explain.'

Francesco was a fascinating man. We talked about all sorts of things: the history of Marina Della Roccia and his family palazzo; the difficulties of the wine-making business; the best recipe for spaghetti alla carbonara. We finished our drinks, ate lunch and ordered coffee, forgetting all about wabi-sabi.

The next day was so stinking hot I gave in and went to the beach with the others. Draped carefully in thin layers of flowing cotton, I followed them on to the sand. It was a Sunday, and so extremely crowded. I found a place on a lounger beneath a bright striped umbrella and prayed for a breeze. All around me were families, playing in the sand and sharing food. The women caught my attention: Italian mammas that looked like great brown seals basking in the sun. They didn't seem to care if their bikini bottoms dug into their flesh, if the fat of their thighs was dimpled. Stretched out on towels with their children climbing over them, or splashing into the waves, they were oblivious.

'Come in for a swim,' Shelley urged.

Gingerly I peeled off my layers, revealing my old swimming costume. My legs looked pasty, so I held on to my sarong almost to the water's edge, then plunged in quickly. The water felt cool and the sun baked my shoulders.

Then I spotted Francesco, belly bared, striding down towards the shoreline, all smiles and calling out to me: 'Signora, signora.'

'Damn,' I muttered.

He dived beneath a wave, his swimming shorts slipping perilously, and swam up beside me.

'Buongiorno, Francesco,' I said when he surfaced.

I cowered in the sea for as long as I could, until the tips of my fingers turned white and wrinkled and I couldn't stand it any longer. When at last I walked out of the waves, I was aware of Francesco looking me up and down.

I lunged for my sarong, wrapping it round my waist.

'I'm so pale,' I muttered. 'It's best I cover up.'

He took me to buy gelato, and together we walked the tideline, kicking through the shallows.

'Oh, Francesco, you meant to explain to me yesterday, what is wabi-sabi?' I reminded him.

'Ah, yes. Well, a faded fresco is definitely wabi-sabi. So is the twisted trunk of an old olive tree, a shrivelled autumn leaf and, yes, an old palazzo. Wabi-sabi is the beauty of things that are imperfect. The Japanese thought of it, and I have embraced it.'

Francesco patted his belly and grinned. 'I suppose even this is wabi-sabi, in a way.'

No, I didn't rip off my sarong. I wasn't about to leap about the beach half naked, glorying in my own wabi-sabi. But when I got back to the palazzo, I thought about what Francesco had said. If its walls were freshly painted and everything was mended or new, would the

Castello Della Roccia be more beautiful? Or would it be less? I wasn't so sure any more.

And that night, after a delicious restaurant dinner for two and a couple of bottles of wine, as we sat out on the balcony of Francesco's apartment and he lit candles so that everything seemed softer and nicer, and then he sat close to me and then he, well you know . . . I wondered if I might be a summer person after all.

Someone Got to Eddie

BY IAN RANKIN

*T*hey paid me not to make mistakes. Not that I
ever made mistakes; that's why I was the man for
the job, and they knew it. I was cautious and thorough,
discreet and tight-lipped.

Besides, I had other qualities, which they found
quite indispensable.

He was lying on the living-room floor. He'd fallen
on his back, head coming to rest against the front of a
leather armchair. It looked like it might be one of those
reclining armchairs, you know, with a footrest and
everything, an expensive item. The TV was expensive
too, but then I don't suppose he ever went out much.
They don't go out much, people like him. They stay
indoors where it's safe. The irony of this being, of
course, that they become prisoners in their own homes,
prisoners all their lives.

He was still alive, breathing badly through his wet
nose, his hand sort of stroking the front of his T-shirt.
There was a big damp stain there, and it was all his.
His hair had gone grey in the past year or so, and he'd
put on a lot of weight.

His eyes were dark-ringed from too many late nights.

'Please,' he whispered. 'Please.'

But I was busy. I didn't like interruptions. So I stabbed him again, just the twice, probably in his abdomen. Not deep wounds, just enough to give him the hint. His head slouched floorwards, tiny moaning sounds dribbling from his lips. They didn't want a quick, painless death. It was in the contract. They wanted something that was both revenge on him and a message to others. Oh yes, I was the man for the job all right.

I was wearing overalls and gardening gloves and a pair of old training shoes with the heel coming away from one of them. Disposable, the lot of it, fit for little more than a bonfire. So I didn't mind stepping in the small pools of blood. In fact, that was part of the plan. I'd put the overalls and gloves and trainers on in his bathroom. This was just prior to stabbing him, of course. He'd been surprised to see me coming out of the bathroom looking like that. But of course it hadn't dawned on him till too late. Always watch your back, they say. But the advice I'd give is: always watch your front. It's the guy you're shaking hands with, the guy you're talking to who will turn out to be your enemy. There aren't monsters hiding in the bushes. All they hide behind are smiles.

(Don't worry about me, I always ramble on when I'm nervous.)

I got to work. First, I dropped the knife into a plastic

bag and placed the package in my holdall. I might need it again, but at this stage I doubted it. He wasn't talking any more.

Instead, his mouth opened and closed soundlessly, like a fish in an unaerated aquarium. You hardly knew he was in pain. Pain and shock. His body was going to wave a white flag soon, but the brain was taking a little time to understand. It thought it was still in the foxhole, head down and safe.

Aquariums and foxholes. Funny the things that go through your mind at a time like this. I suppose it's to shut out the reality of the situation. Never mind virtual reality; this was visceral reality.

I was keeping the gloves on for the moment. I walked around the living room, deciding how the place should look. There was a table in the corner with some bottles and glasses on it. They could go for a start. Hold on, though, some music first. There had been no indications that any neighbours were at home – I'd watched outside for an hour, and since coming in had been listening for sounds – but all the same. Besides, music soothed the soul, didn't it?

'What do you fancy?' I asked him. He had a cheap little midi system and a couple of dozen CDs and tapes. I switched the system on and opened the drawer of the CD player, slipped in a disc, closed the drawer and pressed 'Play'.

'A bit of Mantovani,' I said needlessly as strings swelled from the small speakers. It was a version of The Beatles' 'Yesterday'. Good song, that. I turned the volume up a bit, played with the treble and bass, then went back to the corner table and swept all the stuff on to the floor. Not with a flourish or anything, just a casual brush of the forearm. A couple of wine glasses broke, nothing else. And it didn't make much noise, either. It looked good, though.

The sofa was next. I thought for a moment, then pulled a couple of the cushions off, letting them drop to the floor. It wasn't much, was it? But the room was looking cluttered now, what with the bottles and cushions and the body.

He wasn't watching any of this, though he could probably hear it. His eyes were staring at the carpet below him. It had been light blue in colour, but was now looking like someone had dropped a mug of tea (no milk) on it. An interesting effect. In the films blood always looks like paint. Yes, but it depends what you mix it with, doesn't it? Red and blue would seem to make tea (no milk). Suddenly I felt thirsty.

And I needed the toilet too. There was milk in the fridge. I poured half a carton down my throat and was putting it back in the fridge when I thought, what the hell. I tossed it towards the sink. Milk splattered the work surfaces and poured on to the linoleum floor. I left the fridge door open.

After visiting the toilet, I wandered back into the living room, took the crowbar from my holdall and left the house, closing the door after me. Checking that no one was around, I attacked the door jamb, splintering wood and forcing my way back inside. It didn't make any noise, and looked pretty good. I closed the door as best I could, tipped the telephone table in the hall on to its side and returned to the living room. His face was on the floor now, deathly pale, as you might imagine. In fact, he looked worse than a few of the corpses I've seen.

'Not long now,' I told him. I was all but done, but decided maybe I should take a recce upstairs. I opened his bedside cupboard. Inside a wooden box there was a wad of folded banknotes, tens and twenties. I slipped off the rubber band from around them, chucked it and the box on to the bed and stuffed the money in my pocket. Let's call it a tip. It's not that I wasn't being paid enough, but I knew damned fine that if I didn't pocket it, some dozy young copper first on the scene would do just the same.

It was a pretty sad little room, this bedroom. There were very few decent clothes in the wardrobe, a couple of empty whisky bottles under the bed. No framed photos of family, no holiday souvenirs, no paintings on the walls.

He'd been on medication. There were four little bottles of pills on the bedside cabinet. Nerves, probably. Informers often suffer from nerves. It comes of waiting for that monster to jump out of the bushes at them. OK, so after they've given their evidence and 'Mr Big' (or more usually 'Mr Middling') has been locked away, they're given 'protection'.

They get new identities, some cash up front, a roof over their heads, even a job. All this comes to pass. But they've got to leave the only life they've known. No contact with friends or family. This guy downstairs, whose name was Eddie, by the way, his wife left him. A lot of the wives do. Sad, eh? And these informers, they do all this just to save themselves from a few years in the clink.

The police are good at spotting the weak ones, the ones who might just turn. They work on them, exaggerating the sentences they're going to get, exaggerating the prizes awaiting them under the witness protection scheme. ('The Witless Protection Scheme', I've heard it called.) It's all psychology and bullshit, but it sometimes works. Often, though, a jury will throw the evidence out anyway. The defence counsel's line is always the same: can you rely on the evidence of a man who himself is so heavily implicated in these serious crimes, and who is giving evidence solely to save his own skin?

Like I say, sometimes it works and sometimes it doesn't. I went downstairs and crouched over the body. It was a body now, no question of that. Well, I'd let it cool for a little while. Ten or fifteen minutes. Now that I thought of it, I'd broken open the door too soon. Someone might come along and notice. A slight error, but an error all the same. Too late for regrets, though. The course was set now, so I went back to the fridge and lifted out what was left of a roast chicken. There was a leg with some meat on it, so I chewed that for a while, standing in the living room, watching through the net curtains as the sun broke from behind some cloud.

I stuffed the bones into the kitchen bin. I'd stripped them clean. I didn't want to leave behind any teeth marks, anything the forensic scientists could begin to work with. Not that anyone would be working too hard on this case. People like me, we're seldom caught. After a hit, we just melt into the background. We're as ordinary as you are. I don't mean that we seem to be ordinary, that we make a show of looking ordinary, I mean we are ordinary. These hitmen and assassins you read about in novels, they go around all day and all night like Arnold Schwarzenegger. But in real life that would get them noticed. The last thing you want to be if you're like me is noticed. You want to blend into the scenery.

I'm running on again, aren't I? It was just about time. A final lingering inspection. Another visit to the toilet. I checked myself in the bathroom mirror. I looked fine. I took my clothes back out of the holdall and stripped off the overalls, gloves, trainers. My shoes were black brogues with new soles and heels. I checked myself again in the mirror as I knotted my tie and put on my jacket. No telltale flecks of blood on my cheeks or forehead. I washed my hands without using soap (the fragrance might be identifiable) and dried them on toilet paper, which I flushed away. I zipped the holdall shut, picked it up and walked back through the living room ('Ciao, Eddie'), into the small hallway and out of the house.

Potentially, this was the most dangerous part of the whole job. As I walked down the path, I was pretty well hidden from view by the hedge, the hedge Eddie must have considered a comfort, a barrier between him and prying eyes. At the pavement, I didn't pause. There was no one around anyway, no one at all, as I walked briskly round the corner to where I'd parked my car, locked the holdall in the boot and started the engine.

Later that afternoon I returned to the house. I didn't park on a side street this time. I drew right up to the kerb in front of the hedge. Well, as close as I could get, anyway. There were still no signs of activity in any of the other houses. Either the neighbours kept themselves to themselves or else they all had places to be. I gave my engine a final loud rev before turning it off, and slammed the door noisily after me.

I was wearing a black leather jacket and cream chinos rather than a suit, and different shoes, plain brown rather than the black brogues. Just in case someone had seen me. Often, witnesses saw the clothes, not the face. The real professionals didn't bother with hair dyes, false moustaches and the like. They just wore clothes they wouldn't normally wear.

I walked slowly up the path, studying the terrain either side, then stopped at the door, examining the splintered jamb. The door was closed, but suddenly swung open from inside. Two men looked at me. I stood aside to let them pass and walked into the house. The telephone table in the hall was still lying on its side, the phone beside it (though someone had re-placed the receiver).

The body was where I'd left it. He'd been so sur-prised to see me at his door. Not wary, just surprised. Visiting the area, I'd explained, thought I'd look in. He'd led me into the living room, and I'd asked to use his loo. Maybe he wondered why I took the holdall with me. Maybe he didn't. There could have been anything in it, after all. Anything.

There were two men crouching over the body now, and more men in the bathroom, the kitchen, walking around upstairs. Nobody was saying anything much. You can appreciate why. One of the men stood up and stared at me. I was surveying the scene. Bottles and glasses everywhere, cushions where I'd dropped them, a carpet patterned with blood.

'What's happened here?' I asked unnecessarily.

'Well, sir.' The Detective Constable smiled a rueful smile. 'Looks like someone got to Eddie.'

Fruitbat

BY CARA ROSS

Winner of the woman&home short-story competition

She takes the quickest route, running up the steep steps at the side of Calton Hill, stopping at the railings to catch a breath, calm her pulse and take in a misty winter Thursday in Edinburgh. The view's not brilliant from here.

It would have been nicer to wander slowly up the hill from the other side, and savour her favourite city. But what was supposed to be a breakfast meeting just went on and on. Late, seems like she's always late these days.

She sighs, turns and starts the last flight, but there's no quelling the butterflies in tackety boots that've suddenly started fluttering and dancing somewhere round her middle. Breathe, Ella, breathe. She's going to be pink-cheeked and gasping by the time she gets to the top – not a good look.

James. They'd found each other on a 'married and looking' dating site she'd joined one dull evening when she was working up here for a couple of months. Running her own PR agency means she's quick with words, and her witty, deprecating profile had attracted a full page of replies. She'd been surprised to find so many, even if they were mostly from sad guys who hadn't twigged that it was a way with words that'd get her attention, not a blurry photo of their most outstanding asset.

James is different from the start. His messages are dry, witty, usually irreverent. He teases and taunts, inventing ludicrous stories about things she's doing in her daily life. His stated aim is to get her to call him a git by elevenses each day. He rarely fails. He's a spectacularly dull accountant, he claims, drives a Skoda, plays golf, takes his morning latte at home where he works as a management consultant.

Her first really big corporate client means she's working hard by day, doing overtime in a swish Edinburgh hotel by night. She critiques his website for fun and sends him a couple of pages of hints, to his mock horror. He gives her advice on handling a tricky finance director, about her audit, about difficult clients.

They correspond humorously through a brief but painful hospital stay for her, a family cruise on the Med for him, work appointments in London and Bristol and Bradford and Durham. On one memorable occasion they'd been within a hundred yards of one another, he in a coffee shop near her office, she unable to get out of her meeting.

They often speculate on how things will go when they eventually meet up for coffee and a bun. His proud, penny-pinching Scottish ancestry, he claims, will preclude any chance of doing the gentlemanly thing with the bill. Her natural reticence, she counters, will render her silent: they'd have to communicate in mumbles, grunts and, in extremis, by text.

She reaches the top of the hill, stops for a minute. He's described himself as looking like a pint of Guinness – all in black with grey spiky hair. And there he is. Taller than she'd thought, a bit less geeky, looking at her with relieved recognition, eyebrows raised as if asking a question and a broad smile.

'Hello. I was expecting to get a text with a photograph of some cold feet.'

'Sorry, sorry,' she flusters. 'Couldn't get out of my meeting.'

He'd promised to respect her nerves and not touch her too soon, but she feels his hand gently touch her shoulder in welcome, then settle in the middle of her back as he guides her towards the view.

Her stay in Edinburgh has fostered a love of the soft Scottish accent that borders on a fetish. She's delighted by him. Woulnae. Didnae. Hadnae. She particularly enjoys the way he says 'three-thirty', and begs him to say it again. They walk slowly through the drizzle. She points out the office she was in this morning, the hotel where she stays – they can see her room from here. He says it's amazing, he's been to Edinburgh so many times, lives only thirty minutes away, but he's never been up here, never realised there was so much space.

To her surprise, her nerves result not in embarrassed silence, but inane chatter. He must think she's an idiot.

She was right about the eye-contact thing, though. Impossible to look at someone about whom she knows so much, and who knows so much about her. If she looks at him now, he might just steal her soul.

He steals her hand instead. Long, cool fingers, no gloves. She takes another deep breath, tries hard not to shake her curly mane and gallop off across the hill, away, away from this man she's never seen, never touched, but who has shown such curiosity about her daily life: new contracts, difficult deals, disastrous dates; who's made her describe the type of kisses she likes to receive (and where) in minute detail, and who makes saucy requests for daily reports on the colour and style of her underwear.

He likes the sound of the purple ones she wears for press briefings and TV, and is delighted to hear that when she's really scared she wears her high gold Italian 'fuck me' boots, just to make sure.

The hill's busy, despite the chill mist. He manages to find a quiet spot, turns her round, tilts her chin till she's looking straight into his eyes. His are serious, and, to her admittedly paranoid eyes, maybe a bit mocking.

'A kiss, then?'

Just the best kiss. He'll later describe it as a stunning, rest-of-the-world-disappearing, bluebirds-tweeting-round-his-head kiss. She just can't believe she's been brave enough to initiate it, but loves the soft warmth that spreads through her, the feel of his teeth on her lip, the way that he wants another, straight away.

After that, it's easier. They wander down the hill, chatting comfortably about business, glorious successes and heroic failures, till they reach what's become her favourite place for coffee with clients. In deference to her eye-contact dilemma, he says he'll sit alongside, not opposite.

'Then I can fondle your knees . . .'

She notices his nice way with the waitress, a world away from the embarrassing, dismissive curtness that's been so often displayed at the business lunches she has to attend. It's only later she discovers that he's left-handed. Their seating position means he's eaten his soup with his right to avoid crowding her. She feels cherished, cared about. An unusual feeling.

The bill comes and she pays, laughing that she's cancelled coffee twice already, so she owes him this one. Anyway, she doesn't want to put him in the embarrassing position of having moths fly out of his wallet – it'd harm her image to be part of such a Scottish cliché – there might be clients watching. She checks the time, checks her phone, asks quietly: 'What would you like to do now? Or do you need to get back?'

'Really? What I'd really like to do is take you where I can kiss you some more. Can we do that?'

They'd been firing off emails and texts for three months. They've spoken on the phone. She knows where he lives, where he does business and it all checks out. It feels pretty safe, and anyway, she has a good feeling about him. She can't believe she's doing this, but she walks him to her hotel room.

Funded by the big bank employing her, it's on the top floor, spacious, with massive floor-to-ceiling windows and a view of the hill where they met. It also holds, she realises just a minute too late, a huge, huge bed that at that moment seems to fill the room.

'Wow. Some room.'

'I'll just clean my teeth.'

She escapes to the bathroom so that she can breathe, leaving him leafing self-consciously through a magazine. She noticed his hands shaking. Can he be nervous?

Ella hasn't ever asked about home. He told her early on that his marriage just stopped working, not his choice. He can't leave but can't imagine the rest of his life like this. Finding someone else isn't easy; it's what's between the ears that attracts him, not that easy to discover on dating sites, and he doesn't want to stray too close to home. She's told him that she's currently single after the end of a long relationship. Her life's complicated, busy, and she's been too tied up with work to try.

She's back, minty-mouthed and nervous. His hard kisses seem to make her melt inside, his hand moving up and down, up and down her side. They've shared lots of flirty texts about whether he has a fluffy tummy for her to stroke, one of her favourite things. She pulls his shirt out from his jeans and slides a hand across his stomach. Yep, fluffy: she strokes gently as she unbuttons his shirt; James, meanwhile, seems very keen to get an on-site sitrep on today's underwear.

And then it's easy, easy, easy. Rolling and kissing, touching and licking, each draping legs and arms over the other, they seem to fit together perfectly, laughing, comfortable, tender together. They leap nervously apart as someone tries the door, then collapse in giggles at the thought of two middle-aged people frisking nakedly in the twilight of a murky Thursday afternoon.

He's told her that flaws are what make people perfect, so he traces with his fingers her appendix scar, a childhood gash on her knee, the tiny recent surgery site at the base of her spine, still pink, a long, deep scar under her right arm that she doesn't want to talk about. He declares her perfect in every way.

He showers carefully, says he won't kiss her goodbye because he hates goodbyes and they'll meet again soon. Jingles his car keys impatiently as he descends in the lift. He'll be late, it's his turn to cook, his wife won't be happy. But who'd have thought his Ella would be so passionate, so willing this first time? Driving home, he stops to send her a text. *Chambermaid says hi . . . and what were you up to at 4.30?*

She fills a deep bath, singing happily to herself. She'd expected to feel shy but he made it all fine. She slips into her cosy pj's, fishes a mobile out of her bag. Creatures of routine, they'll be concerned she hasn't phoned at the agreed time. She readies her apology. *Late out from a meeting – a pain.* She comforts herself it's not really a lie.

They agree ground rules. No hurting, no using, no lies. They don't belong to one another, they never will, but what they have can be special. No nosing around; what they choose to tell is what they know about each other. And at the end, a quick decision, a proper goodbye, not a lingering death.

'Nae problem, hen,' he says, grinning.

He sends her beautifully described virtual gifts almost every day. Warm scarves knitted carefully from tender hugs because she hates flying, waiting with her boarding pass. Raspberry kisses that will fizz out of her bathroom taps when she cleans her teeth each morning.

She has new confidence, wins new contracts. She knows she needs to work hard, keep busy, but she finds herself smiling more, hugging herself with the delight of knowing someone cares.

He texts to say he'll be in London on business just before Christmas. He knows she's busy, but does she have any meetings she can move to be there too?

She dithers for ages, trying to decide whether to shyly knock on the door of a London hotel room or just go home. Surely this isn't who she is? A woman with a married lover. She walks slowly down Holland Park Road and the wind makes her decision for her, blowing her closer to him and his hard hugs, long nuzzles, deep kisses.

He can't possibly know the delight for her of walking hand in hand along a busy street. Eating out, sleeping close, like a proper couple. She feels the warmth of him curled around her back, and wakes to find him beside her, his arms wrapped round himself like folded wings. He looks like a sleeping fruitbat, she tells him, and is rewarded with a kiss.

They've discussed their Christmas plans – busy time for him, quiet for her.

They agree a holiday purdah, no calls, but her phone beeps on Christmas Eve with a text indicating a voice-mail. Her special present, it says, not to be opened till Christmas morning. She's in her warm bed when she listens to festive music and his soft, familiar voice.

'Good morning sweetheart, and a very Happy Christmas to you. I'm sitting here at my desk thinking fondly of you cuddled up cosy and warm in your bed with the special people you love around you. You're such a lovely Christmas present, Ella. Just knowing you're there is the best gift I could ever have, and today of all days, I wanted you to know how special you are to me. Have a lovely day, sweetheart, enjoy every single moment . . . lots of hugs from your Fruitbat.'

Ella listens once, twice, once again and smiles. Gets on with folding his clean clothes into a bag, burying her nose deep into the heap of laundry, inhaling their familiar fragrance. Home. They smell of home. And that's what she hopes he'll remember.

She pads through her quiet cottage in thick woolly socks, remembering a time when the air was full of spices and the sound of their laughter as he stole festive goodies from the cooling rack.

She pulls on his favourite mulberry-coloured cashmere dress and velvet boots, packs up the car. The sky's heavy, looks like snow.

James lets the water flow over him and smiles as he thinks of his wife, his beautiful girl. He heard her leave very early, saw her as she stepped into her lover's car. It's been seven years now, but he loves the very bones of her, and their marriage works in every other way. She'll be back in time for their traditional lunch with the family and kids, happy and smiling. Perfect. His busy holiday, surrounded by friends and family.

Ella buzzes herself in with the familiar code, hands over a heap of jauntily wrapped staff gifts and goes through to his room.

At first, he and Ella laughed when he got clumsy, forgetful, forgot first her birthday, then her name. Then came anger and frustration, and then he seemed to forget that he'd ever loved her at all. She doesn't speak about blood and scars and pain, her struggle to pay the care bills, or the hereditary disease that will gradually take his body, his mind and eventually, his life.

Her Stewart. Her funny, gentle, affectionate husband, still sleeping, as he will for most of the day. Her quiet Christmas with the people she really loves.

The Beach Hut

BY PENNY VINCENZI

*I*t had been the most wonderful love affair. Wild and amazing, begun while they were both still students, Michael and Clara; Michael a writer and a dreamer, much given to penning sweet, silly poems dedicated to Clara, a fashion designer with dreams of becoming the next Vivienne Westwood. Michael would whisk Clara off on sudden romantic idylls; most notably to a windswept beach on the North Cornish coast called Trebewick, where they stayed in a rickety wooden building little better than a beach hut and consummated their relationship for the first time, while the sea roared outside.

And as in all the best love affairs, they promised to stay together for ever, and indeed they had, or for twenty years, certainly; and they still loved each other very much, despite certain changes in circumstance, like Michael becoming a smooth-talking and very successful adman, earning big bucks and with a fondness for five-star hotels, set preferably on the Mediterranean coast, and Clara being the chief buyer for a large, middle-market clothes chain. Moreover, they had a beautiful house filled with stylish things and really lacked for very little.

They had raised three very nice sons, one of whom was at university and two at school, the youngest (by seven years) an afterthought: 'The last time conception was even likely,' Clara was given to saying, rather untruthfully, but wanting to make a point of their flagging sex life: the sex life that had been so wild and wonderful and conducted on beaches and clifftops, woodland clearings and riverbanks, simply because they couldn't wait a second longer, even if it was raining or blowing a gale. And sometimes Clara would lie in bed, as Michael slept deeply and noisily beside her, and think of the little wooden cottage in Trebewick and the guttering oil lamp and the way their skin tasted of salt and their hair had tangled together in the wild wind, and wonder quite how things could have changed so absolutely.

Their twentieth wedding anniversary was approaching; Michael didn't seem even to have remembered it. Clara was not so much hurt as disappointed, and filled with a rather destructive restlessness.

So it came to pass that Steve came into her life. Steve was a young designer whose work she had encouraged and even featured in a couple of major promotions. He reminded her of the young Michael, with his wild curly hair and intense nature; she rather feared she must remind him of his mother. But one evening, over a glass of champagne to celebrate his first big order, he told her he found her extremely attractive.

'You're a lot sexier than you let on,' he added, smiling at her with a strange assurance. 'I mean, why the midi skirt when you have legs like men dream about? And the schoolmarmy updo? You should let it all hang out – would you take out those clips for me, let me see . . .'

Half mesmerised, Clara pulled out the combs that held her hair high on the back of her head and shook out a gleaming, dark brown mane.

'Cool,' was all he said, nodding with satisfaction, taking another sip of his champagne. Shortly after, he went back to the basement flat he inhabited in his parents' house, not yet being successful enough to set so much as a toe on the property ladder, and Clara drove home to the large, immaculate house in Fulham feeling as if some wild west wind was stirring somewhere at the back of her heart.

Time passed; the anniversary drew closer, four months, then three. She dropped hints about it to Michael: 'Oh, yes,' he said. 'Our twentieth, getting nearer, isn't it? Got any ideas?'

It was not, she thought, clenching her teeth, for her to have the ideas.

And so one afternoon, with the anniversary eight weeks away, and the same hints met with the same dull, bland response, when Steve invited her to lunch with him the next day to celebrate a new commission, she accepted with almost no hesitation at all. The next morning, she found herself picking out an above-the-knee skirt teamed with a silk T-shirt that had a tendency to emphasise her nipples and a waterfall cardigan in softest cashmere, and left her hair falling to her shoulders and not a comb in sight.

Lunch was very, very sexy; a dangerous meal at the best of times, with its cover of midday innocence. She found herself almost unable to swallow as Steve's knee nudged repeatedly against hers under the table, and completely unable to stop smiling foolishly as his dark eyes probed hers and he told her she looked 'Yeah, unbelievably sexy'.

Lunch was followed by another lunch another day, and ever more frequent drinks after work; she arrived home late at least two nights a week. Nobody cared; Michael very often worked late too, the housekeeper always prepared the boys' evening meal and when she did get home, she found them as she always did, earphones clamped to their heads, or glued to their computer screens, assuring her they were working on their projects, which, as she tartly remarked, were unlikely to be entitled 'War Zone' or 'Aliens Reach Earth'. However, where once she would have ordered the earphones off and the screens blanked, she smiled vaguely at them and wandered into the kitchen to pour herself another glass of wine, hoping, rather than fearing, to find Michael out.

With three weeks to go to the anniversary, and Michael telling her to 'remind me to book a table somewhere that night', a suggestion that after their drinks she should drop Steve home ('I'm fine, truly, I only had one glass of wine') became a prolonged parking up in a side street. She wondered rather wildly what would happen if they were seen and even challenged (headlines in the paper: 'Top Fashion Buyer in Compromising Situation with Toy-boy Designer'), before abandoning herself to the almost forgotten pleasure of snogging in the car, and the stirrings of the heartfelt west wind becoming a hurricane.

And thus to the inevitable, 'Could you maybe get away one night?', and: 'Maybe, you'll have to let me think about it'; the temptation beyond endurance; the sweet anxiety of the plotting and alibi-planting; discovering a conference far enough away to demand an overnight stay; the glorious piercings of guilt. One night, a few days before the conference and the anniversary only ten days away, she mentioned it to Michael as a kind of test.

'Oh, God!' was all he said. 'I still haven't booked anywhere! Why don't you do it? You always like to choose the restaurant, anyway.'

That did it; he deserved it. God only knew where this relationship with Steve was taking her, but she just didn't care. She wanted to be valued and desired and above all cared about again, the security of her marriage suddenly and shockingly less important.

She was packing her bag (new nightdress, long and floaty to disguise the undoubted southward drift of her boobs and her stomach), richly scented oil for the shared bath Steve had rather graphically pictured for her, some scented candles in case they were not provided by the hotel (booked close enough to the conference to make sense, but far enough away to make any sightings by colleagues unlikely), when she felt a stab of sheer panic. How would she cope with the sex, the demands of a young man who was used, no doubt, to the gorgeous firm bodies and skilful performances of girls literally half her age? What was she doing – who did she think she was?

Then she looked at the two pictures of Michael she kept by her bed – one of the wild-haired, burning-eyed young poet; the other a portrait of the handsome, middle-aged cliché he had become, so careless of the marking of twenty years of marriage that he couldn't be bothered even to book a restaurant table to celebrate it. At that moment, she knew exactly what she was doing, and who she was: a still sexy, still hungry forty-something who was grasping at adventure before it was too late. She picked up the bag.

She went down to the hall, left the note she had written for the housekeeper detailing exactly what the boys should have for their supper – chicken lasagne, their favourite, and strawberry cheesecake Ben & Jerry's, as she didn't want them feeling neglected or miserable – and was just going to scribble a cool note for Michael saying goodbye and she'd see him the following evening, when the landline rang.

She frowned; hardly worth bothering, no one she cared about would use it, except her mother, and she was the last person on earth she wanted to speak to this morning. Then she thought of the one other person it might be, Janet the housekeeper, calling in sick – please,

please God, no – and went back in and rather tentatively picked it up.

'Mr Wentworth there?'

It was a voice with a burr of an accent; what was it, Devon? Somerset? No, bit more of an edge.

'No,' she said briskly. 'He's at work. I'll give you his mobile.'

'We tried that. No answer.'

'Oh. Well, he must be in a meeting. You could try later.'

'Can't wait till later. We got a day's work ahead, can't afford to waste the time.'

'Well – I don't know what to suggest.'

'Maybe you could help. It's about where to deliver this wood and stuff.'

'The wood? There must be some mistake. We don't have any open fires.'

'It's not to burn, missus.' The voice sounded amused. 'It's to build with.'

'Build what? I don't understand.'

'The hut. The hut by the beach.'

'The beach? What beach?'

'Trebewick. Where he wants this hut built. Only we can't get to it. We can see where he means, but there's no clearing, not really, all overgrown it is, and what looks like half another hut, all crumbling away. It would be two days' work before we can start putting this one up. So is he going to pay for that, or what? We need to speak to him. Otherwise we'll just have to dump this lot and go.'

'Did you say Trebewick?' said Clara. She felt very odd suddenly.

'That's it, yes. Funny old place this is, fair way from the village. Why he wants a beach hut put up here, Lord alone knows. But anyway, that's not for us to argue about. All I know is it's got to be up and doing in a week's time, and that means he's got to OK the extra money right now.'

'Well,' Clara's mind had cleared. 'Well, I think I can say he – he certainly would OK it. In fact, why don't I give you the go-ahead?'

'That'd be welcome.'

'But could you do me a favour, don't call him. Just get the – the hut up, and if he calls you, don't mention we talked. I – I remember it all now and he'll – he'll be annoyed that I've forgotten.'

'OK.' The voice was amused. 'Don't want to cause trouble between man and wife, that's for sure.'

'No. That wouldn't be a good idea at all,' said Clara, smiling.

Ten minutes later she was on her way to work, still smiling. Not before she had texted Steve to say sorry, but she couldn't meet him after all, not tonight, not at all and she'd try to explain later. He'd be a little upset, but not for long. There would be plenty of firm-bodied, sexually skilful girls to console him. And he wouldn't understand her explanation one bit.

The Midsummer Sky

BY KATHERINE WEBB

*T*he party at Marshfield was going particularly well. Dinner service had been seamless, with nothing late to the table and nothing sent back. The guests had toasted the newly crowned King George V so many times that their eyes were either sliding out of focus, or were too sharp, fever bright. There were lipstick smudges on teeth and glassware; crimson blooms in the men's cheeks; a pervasive aroma of sweat and perfume gathering over the party. The racket of conversation grew louder and louder as the minutes passed. Agnes stood at the top of the back stairs and listened. The kitchen was clear and the bed-rooms ready. The servants were all poised to remove the debris of the meal as soon as it was over; attentive, obedient, everybody sure of where they should be and what they should be doing. But Agnes wasn't feeling attentive, or obedient. A dangerous new voice was whispering in her ear and she heard it clearly, in spite of the noise.

It was another warm, sticky night. The summer of 1911 felt bedded in already, though it was still only June.

The spring had been balmy and bright; hotter than was usual. Cook muttered about it being unnatural, a sign that the world was changing, going overripe and starting to rot. They were all used to her dire predictions, but something about this one rang true. As if change was a strange and worrying scent, carried on the breeze. Agnes knew it was true as she wiped her clammy brow with her fingertips and then lowered her hand into her pocket, feeling around until her fingers found it. Hard, cool, reassuring. Change was coming. She closed her hand around the metal object and felt it nestle into her palm as if it knew her.

Finally the party went on to the terrace for fresh air and the pièce de résistance of the evening – which the guests assumed was the vast champagne pyramid. But Lord Waterford had planned a surprise. The table was cleared in minutes. Swept, wiped, adorned with fresh flowers and candelabra and garish waxed fruit. With the dirty plates delivered to the scullery maids, there were drinks to carry and more waiting to be done for the upstairs maids. Agnes crossed softly to the French windows, to peep out at the guests in their dinner suits and silk dresses and glittering jewels. She thought about John Radley.

He was dining with his parents tonight. They were plain, humble people, lined and callused by long lives spent working. There had been a fete in the village for all and sundry – a gala where the everyday folk could mark the coronation with gossip and the playing of foolish games, and by drinking themselves sluggish on brown ale and cider. By dancing clumsy steps to an oompah band, crushing the daisies underfoot as they went. John had gone to it with Benjamin, with whom he worked, and his brother Kit. The whole village had gone – and several other villages besides. But not the staff of Marshfield, or of the other big houses around, who were hosting parties of their own. Nobody had even bothered to ask if time off might be possible – not with a house full of guests. Thinking about it made Agnes's pulse rise in protest; made her clench her teeth together. The cage around her was invisible, but no less impenetrable for all that. Until now, that was. Until now.

John was a tailor. He'd come to the house to measure the butler and footmen for new uniforms, and even though Lady Waterford hadn't believed that any tailor outside of London could do a satisfactory job, Lord Waterford was swayed by his prices, and they'd both been pleased with the quality of his work. Word was spreading, around the upper classes, that John Radley was the man to go to to dress your servants. He'd recently opened a new shop in bigger premises in town. And while he was at Marshfield, measuring, he'd noticed Agnes, and Agnes had noticed him. He was tall and thin, with elegant hands. The tips of his fingers were hard and leathery from years of working with needles and fabric. He was diffident; he had a long, lean face that could look sorrowful until he smiled. His smile could brighten a cloudy day. It lit up his eyes and made them shine. It made Agnes shine, when he turned it on her – that was how it felt.

Agnes adjusted her eyes so that her own reflection in the glass came into focus. In the borrowed light, there were hollows under her eyes and in her cheeks. Her hair had gone limp from the heat and a wisp had escaped from her cap to hang lifelessly over her forehead. There was still shape in her top lip, but it was thinner than it once was. She was no longer young, and no mistake. Given up by most, including her own mother, as a spinster. She would be thirty-six at her next birthday, and when she lifted her hair to brush it, she found grey strands at her temples, weaving through the brown.

She'd been a child when she first came to Marshfield, just thirteen years old. Taken on as a scullery maid, she'd been promoted to kitchen maid, then parlour maid and now chambermaid. Lady's maid to the Waterford daughters, in all but official title. Play your cards right and you might have my job one day, Mrs Dodd, the housekeeper, told her once. Which was tantamount to saying, you might have my life, with all its long hours and pinched lips, all its disappointments and nothing new, ever – no change, no love. Mrs Dodd had meant it kindly, but Agnes had struggled to swallow the lump in her throat. She wanted more, better, different. She wanted life.

Mrs Dodd walked right out of her thoughts behind her, and Agnes turned quickly to face her.

'Stop dilly-dallying at the window, Agnes! They

won't start for a while yet, and you're needed upstairs,' she said brusquely.

'What's happened?' asked Agnes, as they took the stairs together. She kept her hand in her pocket, squeezed the treasure there tightly. It was her freedom, she told herself. Here was the means, and change was coming. Mrs Dodd shot her a dark look.

'Miss Lillian is . . . unwell, again,' she said, and Agnes understood her at once. 'Megan has already taken a basin up to her, so at least you'll not need to strip the bed tonight.'

'We can hope not, at least,' Agnes muttered. Lillian was the second Waterford daughter, nineteen and pretty but always scowling. A spoilt, lazy girl; spiteful at times. She'd already turned down three proposals, scorning the men as weak and useless, though they'd seemed pleasant enough to Agnes. How must it feel to be so free, so wanton and blasé with life? Agnes had no idea. Lillian was sitting up on the bed, her dress creased and stained. Sour smells of wine and bile were rising from the basin in her lap. Her head rolled towards Agnes when she entered the room; she opened bleary, bloodshot eyes.

'Where have you been? I've been waiting for hours! Rinse this out.' She thrust the basin at Agnes, putting one hand to her brow. 'And open the window, can't you? I'm roasting to death.' Agnes did as she was told and fetched a decanter of water. She poured Lillian a glass and tried to hand it to her, but Lillian batted it away. 'Did I ask for any water?' she mumbled, slurring the words. 'Daddy's furious,' she sighed. 'I told him that if his party wasn't so wretchedly dull, I wouldn't have to drink so much in order to endure it.'

'I imagine that wouldn't help to improve his temper, Miss,' Agnes said, neutrally. She gazed over at the window, where she could see torches lining the drive-way, dancing merrily in the darkness. Wretchedly dull. Lillian had no idea. Dull was missing out on any celebration at all. Dull was doing the same thing day in, day out, with no hope of reprieve.

'You're not here to imagine, Agnes,' Lillian snapped. 'Oh God . . .' she moaned. Agnes held the china basin up to her chin and tried not to grimace.

After John had been to Marshfield a few times, to retake lost measurements or deliver fabric samples, Agnes saw him around more and more. Then he asked her to meet him for tea one Sunday afternoon, and she went, and after that they met every Sunday. The weeks seemed to grind by, stretching longer now that she had even more reason to yearn for her half-day off. John took her face in his hands and didn't see its lines or tired expression. He held her and didn't notice that her breasts had lost their bloom, that her figure was hard and muscular from so many years of labour. She was no soft young peach of a girl, but that was how he made her feel because that's what he seemed to see. He saw something lovely; and Agnes was amazed because she'd never loved a man before, and the riot of nerves and delight that came on when she saw him was utterly alien to her.

'I want to have a child, Agnes,' he whispered to her, clasping her hands in his, and she'd been so startled and happy that words left her. In her heart they sang out: It's not too late.

Outside there was a lull in the party noise, then Agnes heard Lord Waterford make an announcement, and there came a gasp. It's time, she thought. The other staff would be gathering at the French windows – they had special permission to do so. But Lillian's room was at the side of the house, and Agnes would get no view.

'Miss Lillian, I was hoping I might go out for a moment, to watch the—' she started to ask, but Lillian cut her off.

'Oh, do be quiet, Agnes, my head's pounding. Come and take these pins out of my hair.' Agnes stared at the girl, crumpled like a handkerchief on the bed. She stared and dropped her hand into her pocket again, to grasp the talisman there. Now was the time to choose, she decided. The old life, or the new. Without thinking twice she turned and left the room, closing the door softly behind her, hoping Lillian wouldn't realise at once that she'd gone. This profound act of insurrection should have frightened her, but she felt quite calm.

She climbed the attic stairs briskly and went along to Jessica's room, where the windowsill outside was wide. She knew where she wanted to be, for what was to come. She stood on a chair, climbed out through the window and moved along the sill to a ladder that led on to the roof. After twenty-three years, she knew all of the house's secrets. She tried not to see the dizzying ground, wheeling beneath her; tried not to notice the way it spread its arms as if waiting for her. The roof tiles were still warm from the day. Agnes went around to the front of the house, above the terrace where there was now an expectant hush from the guests. Lights glanced from the crowd, from their many colours; from high up and far away they looked glorious, like some heavenly horde.

Agnes tucked herself against a chimney stack, safe and secure. She took the ring from her pocket, slipped it on to her finger and smiled. She'd been waiting for the right moment to tell Mrs Dodd, but now she realised that there could be no wrong moment. When she went down from the roof, everyone would know. Lillian would be cursing and calling for her, threatening her with dismissal. But Agnes no longer cared, or feared such threats. The future was a very different place now. John had asked her to marry him, and she had said yes. She felt such a glow that she was surprised no one had noticed. She wondered if she was pregnant already – if that was what this feeling of swelling up was, of buoyancy, of being about to burst. She held out her hand and admired the ring – plain, honest, decent. Just like he was. She would wear it from now on, and never take it off.

Above her came the most almighty bang, and Agnes tipped her head back to see. The sky was like a warm, living thing; all indigo-dark and soft as velvet, with stars strewn like sequins. Lord Waterford's fireworks exploded across it: plumes of red and gold and silver sparkles that made the stars grow pale and drew dazzling patterns of light. Nobody had a better view of them than Agnes, not even Lord and Lady Waterford themselves. And Agnes felt as though it was all for her – a celebration of her release, of what was to come. Of things that would happen for her now, when she'd given up hoping that they would. She was the midsummer sky, and the bright colours and the splendour were the contents of her heart, streaming out – the wonder of change, and love and freedom.

The Coffee Shop Book Club

Breast Cancer Care is here for anyone affected by breast cancer. We bring people together, provide information and support, and campaign for improved standards of care. We use our understanding of people's experience of breast cancer and our clinical expertise in everything we do.

Every year more and more people need our support. By buying this book, you are helping us to be there for every one of them. We are also enormously grateful to Orion Books and *woman&home* for their generous support in bringing this book to you.

If you would like more information about our work, you can visit www.breastcancercare.org.uk or call our free helpline on 0808 800 6000.